Bride

Of the

Haunted Manor

By

Sephyrra

Wither & Rune Press
www.authorsephyrra.com
contact@authorsephyrra.com
newsletter@authorsephyrra.com

.

Trigger Warnings

Bride Of The Haunted Manor: A Gothic Romance Novella by Sephyrra is a gothic novella with paranormal themes. The book contains content that may be sensitive and triggering for some readers. Please be aware that this book includes:

Adult themes and situations.

Scenes depicting attempted non-consensual situations.

References to child death.

Explicit adult content and scenes, including a foot kink.

Reader discretion is advised. If you find any of these themes distressing or uncomfortable, we recommend considering whether this book is suitable for you. It is essential to prioritize your emotional well-being while reading.

Please take care and make an informed decision before proceeding with this book.

Author's Note

Hey there!

Welcome to "Bride Of The Haunted Manor." This novella is all about adding a dash of excitement to your reading journey. It's here to celebrate our inner adventurers, especially those fabulous ladies who are 35+ and embracing their plus-size beauty.

So, grab your go-to snack, get cozy, and let's embark on a thrilling adventure where monsters and desire come together. It's all in the spirit of fun, and I truly hope you savor every page of this escapade.

Here's to unexpected romance, unforgettable stories, and a spooktacular Happy Halloween,

Sephyrra

A Gothic Love Tale

In Blackwood's dark and ghostly keep,
A love story, eerie, secrets deep.
She, a mortal, he from the past,
In Gothic shades, their love held fast.
In moonlit halls where phantoms roam,
Their haunted hearts found a spectral home.
A century's chasm, no obstacle here,
In the realm of shadows, they drew near.
Their love, a whisper 'midst the chilling air,
In Blackwood manor, the haunting lair.
A ghostly romance, both strange and grand,
In the manor's grip, forever they stand.

Prologue

THE AUTUMN EVENING carried a sense of intrigue, thick in the air, as I tiptoed down the hallway. In my hand, I held a bobby pin, my tool of choice for the task ahead. I was edging towards the door my mother had always declared out of bounds. The mystery behind it had sparked my curiosity, leading me to learn the crafty art of lock-picking.

Meanwhile, in the sitting room, my mother and some of her friends were deeply engrossed in a spirited discussion about the recent sinking of the Titanic and I silently hoped they would continue their lively chatter, giving me the distraction I needed for my secret mission.

Our home stood far from London's bustling

center, in a secluded community that the world saw as a haven of healers. But the truth was a bit more extraordinary – we were witches. Magic ran in my family's blood, though my own magical powers were still a mystery, waiting to make themselves known.

Great Aunt Elara, the coven's matriarch, was an enigma. There were rumors in the coven about how she practiced a form of magic so dark, even our own kind shunned it—a magic brewed in the very room I was about to enter.

One night, while I was busy playing with my dolls in my room, I heard a scream — so loud and agonizing that my dolls slipped from my hand. I knew where the scream had come from— The room Great Aunt Elara used to practice her magic. Leaving my bedroom, I approached the door and pressed my ear against it, listening intently. Before I knew it, my mother's hand clamped onto my shoulder, swift and firm.

"Evelynn," she'd urgently whispered, "that room is not for you."

My curiosity had boiled over. "Why, Mama? What's inside?"

Her eyes clouded over, "Some things are better left unknown."

That piece of motherly advice had done little but fan the flames of my curiosity. Hence, here I was, struggling to unlock the mysterious room while constantly checking over my shoulder. I didn't want to get caught. With a final twist and a click, the door yielded. I stepped inside, my heart pounding like a drum in my ears.

The room was awash in light from flickering candles, casting long shadows on the walls. Chalk-drawn pentagrams and indecipherable symbols adorned its stone surface. Then my eyes fell upon it —the podium at the room's center. On it lay an ancient book, its pages whispered to contain malevolent spells. The Grimoire. A trophy of dark arts in the hands of Great Aunt Elara.

The tingling in my fingers intensified when I touched the Grimoire, feeling almost like an electrical pulse. Startled, I pulled my hand back. My eyes then caught sight of a chalice next to the book. Unable to see what was inside it, I stood on my tiptoes for a better look and immediately gagged at the smell and sight of what it contained.

The chalice was filled with blood. It was a chilling confirmation of all the whispers surrounding Great Aunt Elara's dark practices.

Just then, a force knocked me backward with a whoosh of air. I hit the floor hard, the Grimoire now ominously far away from me. The room felt charged, as if I'd broken an invisible seal.

"Who's there?" I asked in a shaky voice, my eyes darting around the dimly lit space. Panic was gripping me. It felt as if its very walls were closing in on me.

Silence, thick and heavy, was the only response. Gathering my wits, I managed to get back on my feet, bracing for whatever was next. I didn't have to wait long. Another whoosh came from behind, sending me sprawling onto the floor once more. I struggled to get up again, but the invisible force knocked me down again. I felt like a puppet, as if some unseen presence was preventing me from getting back on my feet.

"That's enough!" I shouted into the void, feigning a courage I didn't truly feel. The air grew still, as if waiting for something—or someone.

And then he appeared. A boy my age,

materialized inside the chalked pentagram drawn on the floor. His eyes scanned me, as filled with curiosity as they were unsettling.

"Who are you?" The words left my mouth before I even thought them through. In a room full of the eerie, he was a paradox— present, yet otherworldly.

"I don't answer to puny little witches. Leave this place." he said with a bored look on his face.

I clenched my fists, summoning all of my bravado to confront him. "You will tell me," I declared. "I didn't come here after picking the lock for hours just for some boy to tell me to leave."

He tilted his head, studying me as though I were a puzzle. "And why would you venture into a place like this? Are the whispers not loud enough for you?"

I swallowed hard, trying not to let my fear show. "I heard screaming. I needed to see what was going on."

He chuckled, a sound as unsettling as the room around us. "So, curiosity will be your downfall, will it?"

My skin prickled, and the room seemed to grow

colder. I couldn't help but wonder about the extent of this boy's power and how it would fare against my false bravado.

"You look more like you belong in a sickbed than in a witch's den. You're not exactly intimidating," I retorted, hoping my words would lead him to reveal something—anything—about himself.

For a fleeting moment, our eyes met, and the boy chuckled again. "A boy, you say?" His voice carried a mysterious timbre, and then, in an eye's blink, he transformed. Gone was the youthful body of a boy. Now, he towered over me, a fearsome figure whose skin had become deep crimson. Horns erupted from his skull, the sharp fangs in his mouth glistened like daggers, and a thick tail swished in the air behind him, each movement filled with malevolence.

I staggered backward, my heart pounding a frantic rhythm, eyes opened wide in dread and wonder.

"Who.. Who are you?" I managed to stammer out, my voice barely above a whisper.

With a voice that rumbled like distant thunder, he responded, "I am Balfeeral, son of Balthazar. The

Prince of demon kind."

"Why are you here?" My voice was small but filled with genuine curiosity.

"She, that old witch, chained me here, forcing me to do her bidding," Balfeeral said, his voice heavy with despair. "Given a chance, I'd make her pay for the torment she's put me through!" His words radiated anger.

I crept closer, my heart racing but my feet moving on their own. Gently, I touched his arm. "Is it you? The one who cries out at night?"

His gaze locked onto mine, a mixture of astonishment and pain. "Yes, she torments me, forces the screams from my lips."

My brows furrowed with contempt as I spoke to myself more than to him. "The use of 'Great' in Aunt Elara's title now seems ironic, doesn't it?" I muttered.

In response, he let out a mirthless chuckle. "Great... Is she called 'Great'? She practices dark, ancient magic, the kind that demands blood – the blood of innocent girls like you." His words sent a shiver down my spine, and I couldn't help but wonder where the blood came from, although I didn't want to dwell on it. The confirmation that she was using dark magic troubled me deeply, as it could bring ruin to our entire kind.

I gulped, meeting his pitch-black eyes. "What if I can free you? Once you escape, Aunt Elara will lose her grip on dark magic. It seems like a fair trade," I cautiously proposed.

I gulped, meeting his pitch-black eyes. "What if I can free you? Once you escape, Aunt Elara will lose her grip on dark magic. It seems like a fair trade," I cautiously proposed.

His eyes widened. Balfeeral lowered himself, sitting cross-legged, and his gaze locked onto mine, a hint of vulnerability in his posture. "Why? Why would you do this for me?"

My heart swelled with compassion, and I leaned in closer, my body conveying my sincerity.

"Because every soul, regardless of its origin, deserves the freedom to love, to live. Even if that soul belongs to a demon."

His eyes, once filled with torment, now held doubt. "Alright, let's say your intentions are genuine. But the question is, do you possess the ability to free me?"

I pondered his question and then replied, "I can try. I can look for a way to free you."

His lips curled into a half-smile as he leaned in closer, his body showing interest. "What if I guide you in the right direction? See that book there?" he said, pointing to a podium.

I nodded, willing to listen. "Yes, the grimoire?"

He acknowledged my question with a nod of his own. "Ahh, so you're aware of it. What do you know about it?"

I leaned forward, my eyes locked on his. "That it's an evil book, and it's used by those with bad intentions. If Aunt Elara possesses it, it means she's up to no good."

"Yes, but to free me, you'll have to use that book. Just once, and it will be for a good cause. Are you willing?" He spoke, his tone serious and his gaze intense.

I hesitated for a moment, then agreed. "I'll try. But promise me, if it works, you will not harm my coven."

His eyes still locked onto mine, he leaned back slightly, a flicker of amusement crossing his face. "Very well," he agreed slowly.

"Merely saying 'very well' isn't enough. I need your word, your unbreakable vow," I insisted.

His dark eyes sparkled with newfound interest. "How about we seal it with a blood pact? You free me, and I'll stick to your terms. And just to make it more enticing, I'll owe you one. A debt you can call upon when you wish."

"Alright." I said and extended my hand to seal the deal. Instead of grabbing it, Balfeeral brought my hand to his mouth and bit it. "Ouch!" I yelped, pulling my hand back.

"A blood pact needs blood, little witch," he said, amusement in his voice. He then nicked his own palm with a sharp claw, and our bleeding hands met in a firm grip.

"We have a deal," he confirmed, as our mingled blood sealed the pact. "Now, work your magic."

I shifted my attention to the Grimoire that lay open on the podium. Pages filled with unfamiliar scripts and ancient markings stretched before me. As I flipped through the pages, what I saw made my stomach twist. Dark magic was undeniably vile, but I had a purpose. I needed to find a spell that could free the demon. It was then that one word caught my eye: Libertas, which meant Freedom.

"Ah, Latin," I mumbled, my finger tracing the letters. "Lingua potentiae."

He raised an eyebrow, visibly impressed. "You can read Latin? That's rare among your kind."

I looked up and cocked an eyebrow. "It's the language of power, isn't it? Now, let's get you out of here."

Taking a deep breath, I began chanting the words of release, carefully enunciating each Latin syllable. As I did, chains made of fire erupted from the floor, coiling themselves around him like vipers waiting to strike.

My heart pounded. Was I doing the right thing? Was I setting loose an entity that even dark witches wanted bound?

I fought back my doubt, staying focused on the words I read. "Frangere vincula!"

With that final command, the chains trembled, their fiery links shattering into glimmers of light. One by one, they broke, releasing Balfeeral from the cursed bonds and setting him free.

As the last chain disintegrated, overwhelming joy washed over his face, his pitch black eyes once again meeting mine. "You've done it," he whispered, almost in disbelief. "Thank you, little one. I'm forever in your debt. Not just me, but all demon kind."

.

As Balfeeral vanished, a blood-curdling scream shattered the still night, sending chills down my spine. I sprinted outside, my stomach twisted in dread, and found a horrifying scene: Great Aunt Elara's body lay sprawled on the ground, her head severed and lying several feet away from her body. Her face was frozen in an expression not just of death, but of utter disbelief, all framed by a growing pool of dark blood.

I looked up, and what met my eyes defied belief. Night had turned into an eerie day as fire roared, swallowing our homes whole. It devoured the wooden beams as if savoring a feast, reducing everything to glowing cinders. Heat seared the air, painting my skin with its warmth from where I stood. The acrid smell of burnt wood clawed at my nostrils, and the sound of snapping and popping flames overpowered everything.

Yet, as those in the community fled from their

flaming homes, something else unfolded. The fire, fierce and wild, didn't hurt anyone. It circled around people, weaving between them as if it were sentient, sparing them from its wrath.

Although no one was hurt, the damage ran deep, seared into our very essence. Our sanctuary, hidden from the world's scrutiny, had now been reduced to ashes and smoke.

Chapter 1

THE ROOM IN MY house felt cold, its white walls stark and uncaring. I laid there, trembling and overwhelmed by the agony coursing through my body. Mrs. Darcy, a kind neighbor, wiped the sweat off my brow with a gentle touch.

"Is it supposed to hurt like this, Mrs. Darcy? It feels unbearable," I let the words out through gritted teeth, seeking solace in her eyes, which seemed to hold a lifetime of wisdom.

She offered a reassuring smile. "You're stronger than you think, Evie."

I struggled to speak through the waves of pain, finally managing, "I'm trying, but it's just... too much."

With a gentle nod, she said, "Let me have a look." Mrs. Darcy checked between my legs and then, with a motherly tone, added, "The contractions aren't regular, Evie. It'll take some time. Be patient, my child, and find the strength within."

Just then, I heard Mr. Gregory Darcy calling out to his wife from the house next door, thanks to the thin walls. Mrs. Darcy was a genuinely kind woman, deeply in love with her husband. Mr. Darcy was a decent man himself, but seemed somewhat lost whenever his wife wasn't around to guide him.

"Stella, dear, where is tea?" he called.

Mrs. Darcy jumped up, rolling her eyes. "I swear, that man can't even boil water without me. Let me whip up some tea for him; I'll be back in a jiffy." And just like that, she left.

Now, I was alone in that room, with the pain as my only companion. Tears rolled down my face, not just because of the agony I was in, but because I felt alone and helpless.

Lying there in agony, I couldn't help but let my thoughts wander back to the past. The period right after our coven had been destroyed was the first thing that came to mind. I used to be eaten up by guilt, thinking I had somehow caused Aunt Elara's death. But when the coven found a hidden basement, in the aftermath of the fire, filled with bodies, my guilt disappeared. Aunt Elara had been practicing the darkest of art—blood magic—and she had used the blood of children for it. With that revelation, it was clear she got what she deserved.

After we left our former home behind, my mom and I settled into a small spot in London. We got by, doing whatever work we could find. When my mom passed, I felt lost. At least until I met Edward Barnes.

My past with Edward was a tangled mess. When we first crossed paths, I was a naive eighteen year-old, utterly captivated by his tall, striking looks and steady job. He was twenty five, and seemed like the perfect catch. But even as he courted me, claiming to be head over heels, he was sneaking around, having affairs left and right. Each time he'd stray, he'd crawl back, leaving me feeling like a doormat —used and far from special.

However, he changed once he returned from war,

a war that had taken its toll on him, leaving him with the loss of a leg. The charismatic charm he once possessed had faded, and, perhaps due to a lack of other suitors, he proposed to me when I was twenty four. With my mother gone and no one else to lean on, I said yes. I figured a flawed marriage was better than the lonely life of a spinster.

Now, as I was going through the most excruciating pain of childbirth, Edward was nowhere to be found. Instead, it was Mrs. Darcy, our neighbor, who had heard my cries and came running. She was the one who laid me down on the bed, preparing me for what was to come. And even in that pain, I found myself wishing Edward were there.

The next contraction hit me like a sledgehammer and jolted me out of my thoughts. I bit my lip so hard that I tasted blood, desperately trying to stifle a scream. Amid the agony, I heard a whisper, "You're so brave." Relief washed over me, thinking that Mrs. Darcy was back.

I summoned the courage to open my eyes, but I immediately regretted it. The room was now filled with ghostly figures, all women with their eyes glued to me. Some were dressed in attire from times long past,some dressed in more recent wear, and others were in nightgowns. Yet, there was one thing common among them: ashen skin and hollowed eyes that seemed to penetrate my soul. Panic surged within me, leaving me paralyzed and unable to scream.

"Who are you?" I managed to whisper, my voice trembling. "What do you want?"

A woman with a sunken face emerged from the foot of my bed. "I'm Amanda," she whispered, her voice cold and distant. Seated at the edge of the bed, she stared at me intently. "I'm waiting for my baby." Her grin revealed a mouth devoid of teeth, sending a shiver down my spine.

"This is ... my child," I stammered, fear lacing every word.

She tilted her head. "Not for long." she said with a chuckle.

"Please, don't take my baby," I begged, my voice shaking from fear. "Tell me what I can do to help you, but please, not my child."

"We just want a baby. Our baby," another woman's voice said, but it carried a chilling undertone.

"Yes, please, just give us your child, and we'll find peace,"yet another voice whispered. The darkness in the room seemed to close in around me, and fear consumed me.

"I command you to leave me be," I said with my eyes tightly shut, just as my mother had taught me. Those words were my only hope against the darkness, and I kept repeating them, knowing that my baby's life depended on it.

Then, a hand touched my shoulder, and I couldn't hold back my fear any longer. I screamed.

"Quite the set of pipes you've got there," a familiar voice remarked—Mrs. Darcy had returned. I opened my eyes to find everything back to normal in the room, with the gas lamp glowing brightly. There was no sign of the ghostly women who had surrounded me moments ago.

"Sorry about leaving you for a bit," she said kindly as she touched my belly and checked my pulse. "Everything alright? Calm down, your pulse is racing, dear."

My heart was also racing, and I was drenched in cold sweat. "Did you see them? The women?'"

She smiled gently. "It's just you and me in here. Sometimes the pain and the whole experience can play tricks on your mind. Just breathe. You're safe."

Of course, she hadn't seen them. It was a blessing only for me.

But even as she spoke, a feeling of unease lingered. Those women had wanted my child!

I couldn't dwell on them much as another contraction tore through me. Summoning every ounce of strength I had left, I pushed, and finally, the room was filled with the faint cries of a baby.

As I cradled my newborn daughter in my arms, the haunting presence of the ghostly woman from earlier lingered in my mind. I was determined to do whatever it took to protect my precious baby. At that moment, I decided to name her after my mother — Ava, a name that meant life. I hoped she would be the antidote to the death I had witnessed everywhere during moments of pain.

As the first light of morning began to creep in, I felt a small sense of relief. We had made it through the night and I hoped it was the end. Despite the women's desires to take my baby, they had not succeeded. I was determined to protect my child at all costs. I kissed Ava's tiny forehead and guided her searching mouth to my nipple. She latched on instantly and began to feed. As I watched her, my heart swelled with love and pride. I was now a mother.

As I fed Ava, Edward finally showed up. He leaned in to look at Ava, though I couldn't help but notice the strong smell of alcohol on his breath.

"Looks like you managed everything on your own," he said, his words slurred.

Edward took the baby in his arms and gazed at her with so much love that it stirred deep emotions within me. In that moment, I contemplated forgiving him for all his past transgressions, overwhelmed by the tenderness he displayed towards our child.

"She looks just like my mother," Edward declared with a wide smile on his face, prompting me to silently thank whatever higher power was pulling the strings. Even though Edward claimed to love me before we got married, in the few days after our marriage he found my appearance rather ordinary, and grew to dislike the way I looked.

"You're nothing more than a plain Jane, an ugly whore," he would often cruelly belittle my appearance. "I could've done so much better than you. But I'm stuck with you! Count your blessings, woman, I don't kick you out of the house," he had repeated these hurtful words on numerous occasions, each time attacking my self-esteem with his callous remarks.

So, as long as Edward thought the baby didn't take after me, I knew he would continue to love her.

As I watched Edward cradling our daughter, a smile crossed my face. Yet, that smile disappeared when the memory of what had happened just the day before came rushing back. This wasn't the first time I'd encountered spirits. Those experiences began soon after my mother and I moved from our former coven.

One day, as I was riding back from school on my bicycle, I had an accident. I had fallen and injured my knee. As I cried from the pain, the world around me had grown dark. And then ghosts, pale and bloodied figures with grotesque wounds, surrounded me. Some were missing limbs, while others had vacant eyes. A few had blood pouring from their mouths, like silent screams forever frozen on their lips. And there, among them, stood a boy my age, one of his sockets empty, a haunting sight that made me shiver. Then the boy reached out and touched me. His touch had felt real, just like any living person.

Panic surged through me. I felt stuck between the living and the spirit world. It was like I was being pulled in two directions. So, ignoring the pain in my ankle, I pushed myself up and limped home as quickly as I could, my heart pounding in my chest.

When I burst through the front door and spilled out the extraordinary tale, I braced for my mother's reaction. I anticipated a surge of alarm, perhaps a shared sense of disbelief . Yet, what greeted me was an unexpected blend of emotions on her face: a subtle pride intertwined with melancholy. In a soft, reassuring tone, she uttered, "At last, your powers have awakened. It's a blessing.'"

"Blessing?" I couldn't believe it. That word felt so out of place. How could what I had experienced be a blessing? "Mama, one of those ghosts was able to touch me. Isn't that bad?"

She came over and knelt down in front of me, putting her hands softly on my shoulders like she was about to tell me the most important secret in the world. "You must have felt something for that boy, some kind of emotion like pity or sadness. When you feel things like that, the line between our world and theirs gets really thin. That's why he could touch you. My child, as you already know, our family has a long history of strong magic for generations. It was just a matter of time for your powers to manifest."

"So, how do I make them leave me alone?" I asked, my curiosity finally beating out my fear. I wanted to know how to control this, how to feel safe again.

She smiled, warmth returning to her eyes. "Just tell them to leave. Say, 'I command you to leave me be.' They'll listen, you'll see. You've got more power in you than you realize." And just like that, I felt a bit stronger, like maybe, just maybe, I could do something.

With my mom's words in mind, I felt like I'd found a tool, as if I had been handed a map to navigate a world I never wanted to see but one I couldn't ignore.

The idea that I could communicate with spirits, though, lit a small spark in me. Maybe, just maybe, I could turn this strange ability into something good.

So the following day I went back to the place I had fallen. I settled myself there, hoping to see the spirits from the day before. But after waiting for hours, nothing happened and I returned home feeling defeated.

That night, as I lay in bed, I couldn't stop replaying the events of the previous day in my mind, desperately searching for clues. And then, it clicked. I had fallen and hurt myself, and it was during that intense pain that my ability to see spirits started. It was as though pain was the key, unlocking the door to the other side.

With newfound determination, I returned to the same spot, this time with a sewing needle. I knew what I had to do. With trembling hands, I took the needle and, with a quick jab, pricked my own finger. Immediately, pain shot through me, but I welcomed it as a small sacrifice. I was willing to bear this pain if it meant I could bridge the gap between our worlds.

The area around me turned foggy, and the boy with the empty eye hole appeared in front of me. With a shaky voice, I asked him, "Who are you?"

"I'm Timothy. I died over there," he said, pointing at a canal. His voice was heavy with sadness. "I fell and hurt myself, then I accidentally drowned in the canal. My remains are in some bushes not far from here. My mom is still waiting for me. Can you tell her I'm gone? She needs to stop waiting."

He showed me a nearby house, and I recognized it right away. An old lady lived there. She seemed pretty frail. Realizing she must be Timothy's mom hit me hard, made me feel sad.

That's when it clicked. Here was a chance to do some good with this weird gift of seeing ghosts. I could bring peace to Timothy's mom, help her move on.

As I approached the woman's house that afternoon, my heart raced with anxiety. I knocked on the door and waited. When the door creaked open, revealing the elderly woman, I struggled to find my words.

"I met your son," I began.

She stared at me in disbelief. "Are you out of your mind?"

I shook my head, trying to convey sincerity in my voice. "No, I'm not. But he had a message for you. He wants you to find happiness, and to let you know he's no longer with us, in this world."

Her face hardened, and she snapped, "My son will return. Now get out of here, you bothersome child!"

Tears welled up in my eyes as I turned and left, feeling helpless. I couldn't understand why the boy's mother had reacted with anger and denial. It pained me to think she might never find closure.

I needed a way to help Timothy, and then an idea struck me. I wrote a letter to the police, secretly left it at the station, and waited anxiously for days, hoping they would act. Then, one day, they finally did. They searched the place I had mentioned in the letter and discovered Timothy's remains. This sent shockwaves through the neighborhood. The boy's mother had to confront the heartbreaking reality about her son, and her pain was evident for all to see.

People gathered at the site as the remains were being recovered, and I was among them.

Timothy appeared beside me and said, "Thank you. With my mom knowing I'm no longer suffering, I hope she can find peace, and so can I," his face beaming with a smile. Moments later, I noticed him emitting a gentle glow.

Confusion filled the air, and he asked, "What... What is happening?" His puzzled expression mirrored my own bewilderment.

Curious, I inquired, "What are you feeling?"

His voice trembled with wonder as he replied, "I feel like... Like I'm floating. For years, I had felt like there was a heavy weight on me, and now I feel it has been lifted. Thank you, Evelynn. It's all because of you."

And then, in an instant, he vanished, leaving behind an aura of radiance and contentment. The realization filled me with a profound sense of satisfaction, knowing that I had played a part in bringing him peace and sending him to a better place.

However, when the boy's mother noticed me in

the crowd, she stopped her wailing and pointed in my direction. "That girl! She's a witch. She knew my boy was no more! How?"

My mother hurried to my side and clutched me tight. "She's just a troubled child," she cried out, defending me from the crowd. "She's not right in the mind at times and says silly things. Please, let her be."

She pulled me away from the crowd and took me home, her eyes filled with both concern and relief. "Never reveal your gifts to anyone, Evelynn. The world can be a cruel place for those who are different."

I nodded. My encounter with the spirits had left me changed, and I knew that my ability to see the dead was both a blessing and a curse.

Chapter 2

T HE SECOND TIME I saw ghosts was on my wedding night.

Once the wedding festivities had ended and Edward brought me to his home and then bedroom, my heart raced with anxiety. As a virgin, I was both nervous and excited about finally consummating our love. I had heard that it could be painful for women, but no one had given me any advice or guidance. I knew that Edward and I would have to figure it out together.

As I changed into a simple nightdress, I could hear Edward's footsteps approaching from behind. I turned to face him, desire running through me.

"Are you nervous?" Edward asked, taking a seat on the bed.

"A little," I admitted, unable to meet his gaze. I was ashamed of my lack of experience even though I was twenty four.

He leaned in and kissed my forehead, his fingers gently removing the bobby pins from my braided hair. As my hair fell free, I could feel Edward's eyes on me. I blushed under his gaze.

"You look stunning," he murmured, running his hand through my hair.

I leaned back, exposing my breasts as my robe fell open. Edward's lips found my neck, placing gentle kisses as his hands moved up to my forearms, bringing me closer to him. I could feel his muscles tense as he guided me further onto the bed.

He continued to trail kisses up my neck, stopping to whisper sweet words in my ear. I couldn't help but sigh and relax under his touch.

As the passion between us grew, I responded with equal fervor. My nerves began to calm and I allowed myself to become fully immersed in the moment. Edward's hands began to massage me, sending shivers down my spine. As he removed my robe, I felt more exposed than I had ever been before. My instinct was to cover myself, so I hugged my shoulders, but Edward stopped me and gently removed my hand from my shoulders as I attempted to shield myself.

"I adore you," he said, hovering over me with a look of love in his eyes "Are you still nervous, my love?" he asked, taking a moment to look into my eyes.

"Yes, but I want to do this with you. I love you," I replied, clasping his hand in mine.

With newfound courage, I ran my hands up and down his chest and back as he kissed me with increasing passion. As our bodies pressed together, I could feel the desire and heat between us intensify.

Parting my legs, Edward positioned himself at my opening. As he entered me, a sharp gasp escaped my lips, a mixture of pain and surprise. The pain was beyond anything I had ever experienced, and Edward noticed my distress.

"Are you alright, sweetheart?" he asked with concern on his face.

"Yes, yes, I'm fine, just... umm... take it slow," I replied, trying to steady my nerves.

"I'm too far gone; I don't think I can take it slow anymore," he admitted with urgency in his voice, and he pushed against me and the pain was so intense that I couldn't bear to keep my eyes open any longer, so I tightly closed them. Tears rolled down my cheek, because of the agony I was in. And when I finally mustered the courage to open my eyes again, the world around me had transformed.

We weren't alone in the room anymore. All around the bed stood eerie figures. They were ghostly, their faces looked contorted in pain, and their bodies seemed twisted and unnatural, as if they had suffered unimaginable torment. Each one gave off a feeling of wickedness, making me feel a deep, bone chilling fear.

I screamed so loudly that Edward instinctively backed away, his eyes locked onto me. My screams seemed to terrify him, and he stared at me as if I had gone completely mad.

It was on that fateful day that I decided to share my secret with Edward, "There's something I need to tell you."

His brows furrowed, and he asked, fear in his

voice, "What is it, Evelynn? What's going on?"

I took a deep breath, my heart pounding, and continued, "I see ghosts, Edward, especially when I'm in pain. I've seen them since I was a child."

The seconds stretched into an agonizing silence before Edward finally spoke, his words laced with uncertainty, "Ghosts? Evelynn, are you sure? This... this is hard to believe."

I nodded, staring blankly at Edward, as my confession hung heavy in the air. "I swear, Edward. It's true. Yes, I know it's hard to believe but it's the truth," I exclaimed urgently, my eyes darting around the room. "That one, standing near the window, says he was killed during the construction of this house. And that one, over there, sitting at the edge of the bed, Edward, is sneering at me. He wants to watch us! There's a woman here too, she wishes me harm."

Instead of understanding or supporting me, Edward stared at me with wide, disbelieving eyes. I had to do what my mother had taught me in times like this. I gathered my courage and raised my voice, "I can't take it anymore. Leave me be! Leave me be!"

With a sudden whoosh, a gust of wind filled the room, and the spirits seemed to be sucked out of the house. I collapsed to my knees, sobbing from the ordeal.

Edward, still bewildered, looked at me, and I reached out to touch him. But he recoiled, pushing my hand away.

"You're crazy!" he accused, his voice filled with anger and fear.

"Edward, you need to understand," I pleaded, tears running down my face. "I come from a long line of witches. And it's not something I wanted."

"A witch?" Edward shook his head in disbelief. "You're no witch! You're just a mad woman! You've trapped me, Evelynn. No wonder, no one else wanted to wed you! Oh my god, I married a mad woman. I hate you."

From that day forward, Edward began to drift away from me. Once he found me stunning, now he thought I was plain. Soon after, he spiraled into alcoholism, and it was during one of those intoxicated moments that he got me pregnant.

Chapter 3

WITH AVA, LIFE felt complete. I gave my all to motherhood, overlooking Edward's shortcomings. Yes, he frequently lost himself in drink, but he never let us go hungry. And the sparkle in Ava's eyes whenever she looked at him? That kept me grounded. It's why I stayed.

But one day, he crossed a line that I couldn't ignore any longer. I had known that Edward visited whores but bringing one of them into our home, especially with Ava being just twelve years old, was too much.

"Get out!" I yelled at him, my voice shaking with anger.

"You think you can kick me out of my own

house! You unhinged woman!" he spat back, his face twisted with rage, and then he slapped me.

That slap was the first time he laid a hand on me. I stumbled backwards, my cheek stinging from the pain. At that moment, my sweet Ava rushed to my side, terrified.

"Mummy, are you alright? Daddy, why did you hit her!?" she cried out. Tears were running down her face and she clung to me as if she could protect me.

It was then, holding my sobbing daughter close, that I knew things had to change. Edward had gone too far, especially with our precious Ava.

A few weeks later, when Edward was at work, I made a snap decision. I packed our bags and we left that house behind.

At that moment, I didn't have a clear plan, but I knew we needed to escape from Edward's grasp. We hurried into a carriage, the seats providing a comforting embrace. As the carriage wheels began to turn, a gentle rumbling sound filled the air, signaling our departure .

Tears ran down my face, and Ava, my sweet daughter, reached out and gently wiped them away.

She looked up at me with concern in her eyes and asked, "What's wrong, Mummy?"

I sniffled and replied, "Ava, life can be so hard sometimes. Mummy just wants to sleep and never wake up."

Ava's voice was soft and full of love as she said, "You mean... die?"

Realizing I was saying such things in front of my daughter, I wiped my tears and put on a fake smile. "Of course not. Nevermind. Look, the view is so nice." I said pointing at the lake we were passing by.

But Ava's were glued to mine. "Mummy, you think I'm a little girl. I am twelve now. I know things and I know what you meant." she said as she squeezed my hand tighter. "You have to promise me that you'll keep on living. Now we are away from Daddy, and together we'll find happiness. Promise me."

I gazed into her innocent eyes and made a solemn promise, "I promise, sweetheart."

We were nearly out of town when a horse-drawn wagon blocked our path. My heart sank as uniformed men got out of it.

"Is Evelynn Barnes in this carriage?" the police inquired. Fear gripped me, rendering me silent as I averted my gaze, unable to meet their eyes. However when they took out a sketch of my likeness and began presenting it to the fellow passengers, panic welled within me. It wouldn't be long before they'd spot me. Trapped, with no escape in sight, I reluctantly raised my hand. "Yes, that's me." My words emerged softly, their reach hindered by the wind.

I had anticipated that Edward would eventually track us down, but I didn't expect it to happen so soon. My hope had been to reach another town before he knew we were gone.

"We need you to step out of the carriage with your daughter. Now!" The police officer demanded loudly.

As I stepped down, the ground felt rough and uneven. Edward was coming towards us, his face twisted in anger. He slapped me hard across my face and I went crashing down on the ground.

"You crazy bitch! You tried to take my daughter. I'll have you sent to jail!" he yelled, his eyes blazing with rage. He grabbed Ava from me, and she started crying, her sobs filling the air.

Tears welled up in my eyes as I pleaded with the officers, "Please, officers, I was just trying to protect myself and my daughter. He's been hurting me for so long. No child deserves to live in a home where her mother isn't loved and respected." I begged them for help, but it didn't make a difference.as my words fell on deaf ears and the police took me to another carriage. As I sat in there, a heavy weight settled into the pit of my stomach. My world had crumbled in an instant, and I had no idea what to do.

Chapter 4

IN THAT GLOOMY lockup, I couldn't stop my tears. The room felt tiny, and its dull gray walls seemed to close in on me. Other women were there too, a mix of folks who looked like they'd seen rough days on the streets and others like me who might've lived more decently before ending up there.

One lady, seemingly curious, struck up a chat. "Hey, what's your story?" she asked, her eyes focused on me.

Another woman, a bit gruffer, chimed in, her tone accusatory. "You don't seem like you belong here. I bet you decide to get rid of a troublesome husband. Right?" she said, moving towards me and I couldn't ignore the not-so-great smell surrounding her – a blend of body odor and the damp, musty smell that lingered in the lockup.

I scrunched up my nose and moved away from her and that seemed to enrage her.

"So you think you're better than us! Huh!" saying that she spat at me. "Now you're just as dirty as us!"

I shook my head slowly, speaking barely louder than a whisper, "I'm just like everyone else here," I murmured. "Could you please leave me alone?"

But the woman didn't care about my misery. Instead, she gave me a nasty kick before slinking back into the shadows, leaving me alone on the chilly and unforgiving floor. The only thing I had to hold onto was a cold, hard bench. I rested my head on it, clutching my chest as if that would somehow ease my pain. As I cried, the gas lamps outside cast eerie shapes on the walls, making the lockup feel even more alien.

Then, something extraordinary occurred amidst all that gloom. I felt a touch that was gentle and comforting.

I looked up and couldn't believe my eyes – it was my mother. She looked different from how I remembered; she had a glow to her.

"Dear, don't cry," she said with a warmth in her voice.

I did as she said and took a deep breath and wiped away my tears even though the ache in my heart remained. "It hurts so much, mama," I admitted, my voice trembling.

She understood, her compassion shining in her eyes. "I know, my child," she whispered, her fingers brushing gently against my cheek, cool and soothing.

In the midst of my emotional storm, I dared to ask the question that had haunted me. "What power is there in seeing the dead?" My voice trembled.

"In time, my dear, you'll come to understand," she assured me, her words carrying comfort. With a final, tender touch, she faded away.

As I glanced around the lockup, I saw the other women looking at me, their faces filled with disbelief.

"This one's a loony!" one of the women muttered, setting off a round of chuckles. They had no idea what had truly gone down, and it's not like they'd believe me if I told them.

The day of my trial finally came around, and I couldn't help but hope that I might catch a glimpse of Ava, but she wasn't there in the courtroom. The place was quite grand, with tall ceilings and shiny wooden benches that almost seemed to glow under the gaslamp lighting.

Edward was on the opposite side of the courtroom, looking composed, but his eyes told a different story. They were filled with a burning anger that he was barely holding back.

As the whole thing began, Edward's lawyer started throwing venomous accusations my way, and my own lawyer didn't put up much of a fight. It felt like I was swimming against the tide, and deep down, a seething anger was building up.

When it was Edward's turn to take the stand, I just knew he was gearing up to make my life miserable.

"Your Honor," Edward started, his voice laced with bitterness, "I have genuine concerns about Evelynn's mental state." While he maintained an outward composure, his eyes betrayed a deep-seated malice. "She frequently falls into fits of frenzy, and there have been instances when she attempted to harm Ava."

I shivered as I listened to his damning words. My heart raced, and my hands became sweaty. It was clear that Edward was trying to make everyone think I was the bad one here.

Desperation took over, and I begged with all my heart, my voice shaking with emotion. "Your Honor, please understand—I love my daughter, and I'd never hurt her."

But Edward didn't stop there. He kept spinning his web of lies with expertise. "She claims to be a witch, Your Honor," he declared with a cruel smile. "She's dangerous. She claims she sees dead people. I fear for Ava's safety when she's with her."

Edward's words made me feel like I was sinking. My eyes welled up with tears and staying composed was impossible.

I kept pleading my innocence, my voice thick with emotion. "I'm not crazy, Your Honor. Please, believe me." My words echoed in the courtroom.

Edward's lies had taken root, and the judge's decision was quick and final. "Based on the evidence," the judge announced, his tone determined, "I agree with Mr. Barnes. Mrs. Barnes, you'll be sent to a mental institution for evaluation and treatment."

Those words felt like a death sentence. I felt shattered, torn from my beloved daughter and now committed to a mental institution! It was all too much. Too unjust.

As they led me out of the courtroom, I couldn't help but glance at the judge one last time. I clung to hope, praying for any sign of doubt or compassion on his face. But his expression remained unchanging, and my hopes for justice were crushed.

Chapter 5

I N THE DAYS that followed, I received divorce papers from Edward, marking the end of our marriage. Surprisingly, I didn't feel any sadness, but the absence of Ava, our separation, weighed heavily on my heart. Soon, I found myself confined to a plain, cold room within the mental institution. The walls, painted in harsh, icy white, and the strong smell of cleaning chemicals pricking my nostrils with every breath.

This room didn't offer any kind of comfort. It had one window, but even that was gloomy, with those iron bars casting these long shadows on the chilly gray floor. The window didn't give me much of a view, just a tiny peek at the outside world, a cruel reminder of the life I'd been torn away from.

Whenever I dared to step out of my room, the hallway in this place seemed to stretch on forever, and its high ceilings made me feel small and helpless.

As time passed, my good behavior as a patient granted me access to the common area. One quiet day during a break, I found myself deeply engrossed in an old, well-loved book gifted to me by an orderly. Even though I had read it twice before, my affection for the book remained strong. I had a soft spot for romance novels, though I knew such stories were confined to the pages.

Feeling the need to use the restroom, I got up and headed there. Upon returning to the common area, my heart sank. Mark, another patient at the mental institution, was callously tearing pages from my cherished book. His presence left me with an unsettling feeling; he'd tried to flirt with me on numerous occasions, and his intentions never felt genuine.

"Mark, why are you here?" I questioned, attempting to stay composed. "Can I please have my book back?"

His dark eyes gleamed, a malevolent smirk

forming on his lips. "I'll give it back, but you'll owe me something."

I swallowed hard, dread pooling in my stomach. "What are you talking about?"

"Come now, Evelynn," he purred. "You're a beautiful woman. You know exactly what I mean."

Anxiety welled up within me. Looking around, I realized the two of us were alone in the common area. Trying to maintain some semblance of control, I replied, "Keep the book. I'm leaving."

But before I could make my escape, Mark's bony hand clamped onto my wrist, pinning me to the nearby wall. His rancid breath hitting my face as he leaned in close.

"Stay away from me!" I retorted, my voice filled with revulsion.

Mark's features contorted in fury, the worn asylum uniform draped over his skeletal frame, adding to his menacing aura. "You won't deny me!" he hissed, his other hand darting forward.

Instinctively, I struck out, my knee connecting sharply with his groin. He let out a pained gasp, staggering back, his grip loosening.

"You'll regret that!" he spat, his face contorted in

pain and rage, his unkempt hair making him appear even more sinister. Saying that, he hurled himself at me. His wiry fingers scraped against my cheek leaving a fiery sting in their trail, and I let out a scream filled with sheer terror.

He chuckled, tightening his hold. "You think you're too good for me, huh? Let me show you what I can do," he threatened, dragging me towards the window.

Before I knew it, my head was slammed against the glass, and I saw stars. I tried to fight him off, but his thin frame seemed to have gained an unnatural strength. The pain was excruciating, and I could feel warm blood trickling down my face.

Suddenly, the door burst open, and staff poured in and pulled Mark from me.

A nurse came to me and helped me up, her eyes soft with a blend of compassion, ushered me into an adjacent room. As she examined my wounds, there was sadness in her gaze.

"Sweetheart," she said with a gentle sigh, "one of these cuts will require stitches. And it might leave a mark."

A heavy weight settled in my chest. "Does it even

matter?" I whispered, my spirit defeated.

Her hands stayed steady as she started the suturing process. The pain became overwhelming, and in the background, I noticed a group of ghosts watching me. Some wore patient uniforms, while others were in nurse attire. But I didn't pay them any mind.

Despite the nurse's gentle touch, the stark reality of my situation hit me hard when I caught a glimpse of my reflection. The bruised and battered image glaring back served as a cruel reminder of the darkness in my world.

I could tell the ghosts to leave me be, but how could I get the living to do the same.

Chapter 6

I SPENT TWO long, agonizing years trapped within the walls of that mental asylum. The day I was finally released, I wore the same clothes I had been wearing on that dreadful day when I first entered the asylum. The fabric had become worn and faded. But I didn't care about my appearance; all that mattered was the prospect of reuniting with my beloved Ava.

My heart raced with excitement as I boarded a carriage that would take me back to my former home. I couldn't wait to see Ava's face again, to hold her in my arms. She would be fourteen years old now, and I couldn't believe how much time had passed since I last saw her.

As the carriage journeyed on for what felt like

hours, I couldn't help but steal glances out of the window. The familiar sight of the town came into view, and my anticipation grew. However, I couldn't ignore the curious and somewhat judgmental stares of our neighbors. No one approached me or offered a word of welcome; they simply watched me in silence.

When the carriage halted in front of the familiar house, a wave of apprehension washed over me. My hands, shaky and hesitant, knocked on the front door. Each knock mirrored the pounding in my chest.

A voice, unfamiliar and inquisitive, asked from behind the door, "Yes, who are you?"

"It's Evelynn," I said cautiously. "I live here. Is Ava here?"

The door swung open wider, revealing the woman's face. A knot tightened in my stomach. Was she Edward's new wife? Had he remarried after divorcing me and brought her into Ava's life?

"Look, I'm just here for Ava. You're welcome to my good-for-nothing husband," I blurted out.

The woman looked at me like I had lost my mind and then realization dawned on her face. "Oh, you must be the Evelynn we've heard stories about," she said, circling her finger near her temple in a 'crazy' gesture. "Your husband sold us this house and took off."

The woman's mocking gesture stung, but I ignored it because I was worried for Ava. "When did this happen? Do you have any idea where they might be?" I asked as my voice quivered.

"I don't know. Please, don't come again." she murmured, shutting the door in my face.

My knees buckled, and I sank to the porch, gripping the railing as if it could anchor me in a world that had just slipped sideways. My eyes blurred with tears. "Why does this keep happening to me? When does this nightmare end?" I felt like I was shouting into a void, and the void wasn't answering back.

My self-pity was interrupted by the soft sound of footsteps. I glanced up, finding Mrs. Darcy's compassionate gaze fixed on me. She approached and sat beside me, her presence comforting.

"Evelynn," she whispered, a maternal warmth in her voice, "you've endured so much."

I buried my face in my hands, my voice breaking,

"Why is my life filled with such pain?"

With a sigh, she began recounting her own tale of heartbreak, of losing her child years ago, and how the shadows of that loss still lingered. She didn't promise that everything would be okay, but her words, filled with her own pain, offered a shared understanding.

"I may not have experienced exactly what you're going through," she said softly, "but know that I too understand the sting of loss."

With Mrs. Darcy's support, I managed to get up from the porch. She took me to her home, where she gave me a warm cup of tea and some clean clothes. The tea helped calm my nerves, and the fresh clothes made me feel a bit more like myself.

Mrs. Darcy didn't stop there, though. She offered me a small room in her house to stay until I could find a job and get back on my feet. Her kindness made me believe that maybe things would start looking up.

In return for their kindness and hospitality, I did my best to be a considerate and helpful guest. While I couldn't repay them financially, I made sure to express my gratitude through my actions, working hard to make the Darcys' lives a little easier.

On a bright and sunny morning, Mrs. Darcy and I sat in her cozy living room. Sunlight streamed through lace curtains, creating a warm and inviting atmosphere. Mrs. Darcy held a newspaper in her hands, her eyes filled with thoughtfulness.

"Evelynn," she began gently, "there's something here you ought to see."

I leaned in closer, my curiosity piqued. She unfolded the newspaper carefully, revealing an advertisement that had caught her attention.

"It's a job posting for a caretaker position at an old manor, a little far from here," Mrs. Darcy explained, her gaze shifting between me and the ad. "They're looking for someone to look after the place. It could be a great opportunity for you, dear, to have both a place to stay and a job."

I studied the ad closely, my fingers tracing the words that described the manor and its surroundings. It was situated in the countryside, surrounded by lush gardens and dense woods.

Mrs. Darcy's concern was evident as she

continued, her voice filled with care. "Evelynn, I know how much you miss Ava, and your desire to find her is strong. Taking this job might just be the step you need to get back on your feet and continue your search."

I nodded slowly. "You're right, Mrs. Darcy. I have to find stability before I can have Ava back."

With newfound determination, I declared, "I'll apply for this caretaker job. Maybe it will bring me one step closer to my daughter."

A warm smile graced Mrs. Darcy's face as she offered her support. "That's the spirit, Evelynn.

Chapter 7

A
S THE CARRIAGE door swung open, I stepped onto the cobblestone path leading up to the manor. My heart was pounding, but I took a deep breath to steady myself. This was a big deal, an interview that could change my life. I was wearing a new pink dress Mrs. Darcy had given me . The high waist and straight skirt were simple yet elegant, suitable for an occasion like this. My hair was neatly coiled into two buns on either side of my head, a style that took me longer than I'd care to admit but seemed appropriate for the interview.

The gravel crunched beneath my feet as I stood outside the imposing entrance gates. The manor was undeniably grand, but an eerie feeling lingered even in broad daylight. Something about this place was undoubtedly unsettling. I fixed my gaze on the manor, and for the briefest of moments, it felt as if unseen eyes were watching me. I turned around to scan my surroundings, but there was no one in sight.

I hesitated for a moment before mustering the courage to knock on the massive wooden door. The sound echoed in the silence, a hollow noise that seemed to fill the whole place. But there was no response, no sign of life inside. It felt like the place had been deserted for years, left to the passage of time.

I waited for what felt like a really long time, just sitting on a nearby rock. The silence was creepy, but I didn't have anywhere else to go, so I stayed.

Eventually, the distant sound of hooves drew closer until two horse-drawn carriages came to a stop in front of the manor. Men and women in servant uniforms emerged from the first carriage, making it clear that this was no ordinary arrival. The visitor had come with an entourage.

A butler opened the door of the second carriage, and from within, a young lady daintily stepped out.

Her gown was nothing short of a masterpiece, beautifully adorned with lace. Her golden hair glistened in the sun, with the braids on her head resembling a radiant crown. She appeared younger than me, perhaps around twenty-three, making my thirty-eight years feel quite old in her presence.

"I'm Lady Cassandra, and you must be Evelynn," she said. Her voice held authority, and her presence commanded attention.

"Yes, I'm Evelynn. It's great to meet you, Lady Cassandra," I said, curtsying. However, she grabbed my arm and chuckled.

"Oh my, no need to curtsy. I'm not a fan of it," she replied, then linked her arm with mine, as if we'd been friends for ages.

We strolled forward, the heavy wooden door had already been opened by her butler, and when we entered, I saw the dimly lit foyer. Paintings, covered with cloth, adorned the walls, and chandeliers hung from the ceiling, casting intricate patterns of light and shadow. Dust seemed to have settled on every surface.

Lady Cassandra gave me a tour, and I noticed that all the furniture was covered with sheets to protect it from dust. However, the drawing room, where Lady Cassandra led me, had been cleaned by her servants.

She gestured for me to sit, and I settled into one of the comfy chairs. She took a seat across from me, her gaze locked onto mine.

"Evelynn," she began, cutting straight to the point, "you're the only one who's come for the interview. Maybe it's due to the dark history of Blackwood Manor."

"Dark history?" I echoed, puzzled.

"Ah, you're not aware," she continued. "Well, it's my responsibility to fill you in before offering you the job. You see, this manor has been in my family for generations. It originally belonged to my great-great-uncle, Fredrick Blackwood. Over time, it passed to my father. Now, with his health in decline, the duty of looking after the manor falls to me."

I nodded, still not understanding what she meant by 'dark history'.

She continued, "As you can see, it's undoubtedly a magnificent manor. But before we discuss the job, you should be aware of its history. After

Fredrick Blackwood and his family met their untimely demise here, the manor housed various tenants. But after some rather unsettling incidents, it remained empty for quite some time. Many believe it's haunted because of the tragedies that took place here. I, however, see those stories as just that—stories. I believe those past residents simply met with bad luck."

Glancing around, all I could see was a stately manor cloaked in layers of dust, nothing more. "Every place has its history. This one is no different." I said.

"You're correct. However, stories about ghosts and even monsters are the reason this place has stayed empty. Tell me Evelynn, do you believe in ghosts?" she said, leaning towards me.

I fidgeted uncomfortably in my chair, the weight of her question bearing down on me.

Was I a believer in ghosts? Well, I could see them. But, of course, I couldn't let her in on that secret.

"Of course not, Lady Cassandra," I replied with a forced chuckle. "You know how people love to invent old tales and let their imaginations run wild."

Right on cue, a chilling sensation brushed my face, as if cold fingers had delicately brushed aside a strand of my raven hair that had strayed over my eyes. I couldn't help but freeze in place.

Cold sweat formed on my brow, but thankfully, Lady Cassandra seemed oblivious to my inner turmoil.

"Perhaps," she conceded, "but the undeniable truth is that I require someone to care for this place, to prevent it from falling into complete disrepair. The manor may bear a dark history, but it's also a significant part of my family's legacy. I am willing to offer you both a place to reside on the estate and a modest salary. You will have your own cottage nearby."

My heart wrestled with hesitance. The thought of living near a supposedly haunted manor was intimidating. But my choices were limited, and burdening Mr. and Mrs. Darcy with more financial troubles wasn't something I wanted to do. Besides, I didn't have the means to return to town.

Gathering my courage, I said, "Lady Cassandra, I appreciate your honesty and I'm more than willing to accept the job. I really need the work, I might not have a fancy resume but I promise to take good care of the manor."

Lady Cassandra's face softened, and she offered me a warm smile. "Thank you, Evelynn. You have a brave spirit. Then it's settled. We have a new caretaker for Blackwood Manor.

Once I understood my duties, Lady Cassandra explained how she would arrange for supplies and groceries to be sent to me. Her butler then moved my modest suitcase to a charming cottage. It had a bed, a window facing the manor, a small kitchen, and even an indoor toilet. It was small but cozy, and having a place of my own made me happy. Once I was settled, the butler handed me the keys to the manor.

"Before you leave, could you post a letter for me?" I asked the butler.

"Of course," he replied.

I quickly penned a note to Mrs. Darcy, updating her about my new position as the caretaker. When I handed the sealed letter to the butler, he assured me he'd see it posted.

As I stood at the cottage's door, I watched Lady

Cassandra and her entourage slowly disappear from sight. A sense of anticipation filled me. I felt that I was on the cusp of a new and promising chapter in my life.

Chapter 8

EVEN THOUGH I had my reservations about the manor, I had a job to do and over the next few days, I settled into my role as Blackwood Manor's caretaker. Ever since I had joined, I had been rather cautious, making sure I stayed clear of anything that might lead to harm, particularly because of my gift to see spirits when I was in pain. Each morning, I made my way to the manor, my footsteps echoing through its grand halls. The place was massive, and it was easy to get lost in its maze-like corridors and rooms. I spent my time laboring away at the manor and I felt it was a bit weathered but not haunted.

On a sunny morning, I began the task of cleaning the walls and removing cobwebs. As I uncovered the paintings hidden beneath sheets, I came across one depicting a couple. Strangely, the man's face in all the paintings had been scratched out, leaving only a void. However, the woman beside him stood out as a vision of regal beauty. Her doe-like eyes, plump lips, and every aspect of her radiated stunning grace. The man beside her, hinted at a handsome presence that remained hidden.

Once done with the paintings, I started cleaning a grand antique mirror in the entrance, I stopped to look at my reflection. My blue dress, which had been clean earlier, now had dust on it, and there were a few cobwebs in my hair. I couldn't help but feel inadequate compared to the woman in the painting. As I looked at my reflection, my fingers touched the scar on my cheek, reminding me of my time at the mental institute. I stood still, taking it all in.

It wasn't that Mrs. Darcy's house or my own little cottage didn't have a mirror. It was just that here I could see my entire self, from head to toe. Staring at my own image, I couldn't help but see the changes in my appearance. I had never been a conventional beauty, but there had always been a certain charm to my features. Now it seemed that years of sorrow had left their mark on me.

I had always been petite, but at the age of thirty-eight, I had gained a bit more fullness in my figure.

"It's not like you have anyone to impress, Evelynn." I pouted, speaking to my reflection in the mirror. My own playful expression made me giggle.

As I continued my chores, a faint sound in the distance caught my attention. It was a soft but sad piano tune, its haunting notes floating through the air. The hair on the back of my neck stood up and Lady's Cassandra's words about the manor's history ran through my mind. Intrigued more than scared, I wanted to discover the source of the music. After all, I was a witch; ghosts and hauntings didn't easily rattle me.

Following the sound, I entered a room that seemed to be the ballroom of the manor. The moment I stepped inside, the piano music ceased, replaced by an unsettling silence. I looked around, and while the grand ballroom was surely creepy, its captivating allure just drew me in. Antique candelabras adorned the room, their aged charm exuding an enchanting aura. Above, a resplendent chandelier hung, a dazzling masterpiece suspended in time. It was a pity, however, that this magnificent space had fallen into disrepair, shrouded in neglect and dust.

Determined to bring back the faded beauty of the ballroom, I set out to clean it. I began carefully pulling off the sheets one by one, covering the furniture. While wiping the dusty surfaces, I wondered how so much dust could gather even under the covers. But suddenly, my cleaning was interrupted. A small drop of blood appeared on my fingertip. I had pricked it on a wood splinter that I hadn't seen.

The moment the pain registered, the room seemed to spring into action. The furniture coverings floated upward, as if pulled by unseen hands, filling the room with an energy that was hard to explain. Among them, one cover seemed to twist and shape itself into something much more frightening—a human-like form, as if a man were standing there, covered by the cloth. It felt as though the very air was thick with dread, and whatever was under that particular cover was not something or someone I wanted to meet. My heart pounded in my chest, my body frozen with fear. Then a hand—pale and ghostly—burst out from the cloth, holding a knife that had blood stains!

The room froze as a bone-chilling laugh filled the air, making my stomach twist. "You're mine, Chloe!" A voice that sounded like it crawled out of the deepest pit of nightmares, shattered the silence, filling the room.

This was beyond frightening, far worse than any haunted experience I'd had. My mind was yelling at me to get out.

Adrenaline surging through my veins, I made a break for it. The knife-wielding shape seemed to chase me, its rustling fabric filling the room. Just as I burst through the main door, my body collided with something solid—it wasn't a wall, but a person. A startled scream escaped my lips, but before I could fall, strong hands gripped my arms, keeping me on my feet. My heart, however, still pounded wildly in my chest.

As I met the stranger's eyes, I saw a flicker of surprise cross his face. "Run! It's coming! Run!" I blurted out, trying to sidestep him to make my escape. But he held my arms in a firm grip, anchoring me in place.

He cocked his head, his ocean blue eyes shifting to look behind me. Following his gaze, I turned around, expecting to see the terrifying shape. But the shape had now vanished. A shiver coursed through me.

His eyes met mine again. "Breathe. There's nothing behind you. Are you alright? Injured?" His voice was tinged with concern, and as he spoke, his grip on my arms eased just a bit.

"There was–" I stammered and looked behind once again and found nothing. "Yes, I'm quite alright. I think. I just need a minute." I said and quickly locked the manor's door before sitting on the steps outside, attempting to catch my breath. The stranger joined me, and I couldn't help but feel a sense of curiosity.

"Who are you?" I inquired, sitting a little further away to maintain some distance from him.

"I..I..I am Frenchie. I'm the groundskeeper of Blackwood estate. You must be Evelynn. Lady Cassandra told me about you." he said and I narrowed my eyes at him.

"Lady Cassandra didn't mention any groundskeeper working here. I'm quite certain of it." I said, as I stood up.

Frenchie followed suit and stood up, brushing the dust off his pants. "Perhaps she forgot to mention me. Look, she even sent groceries for you," he remarked, pointing to a large wooden crate filled with various items.

I looked at him with suspicion, feeling anger toward Lady Cassandra. If there was a man here, she should have informed me. It wouldn't be proper for him and me to be alone on the estate grounds.

Letting out a breath, I tucked the loose strand of hair behind my ear that was bothering me and went to pick up the crate.

"Can I?" Frenchie moved forward to help, but I stopped him with a wave of my hand, and he leaned against a pillar with his arms folded.

I attempted to lift the heavy crate, but it proved to be a formidable task. It seemed Lady Cassandra had sent enough provisions to last for two or three months. The thought of unpacking each item one by one was daunting.

Glancing over my shoulder, I noticed Frenchie observing me, his head cocked to one side. I sighed, realizing I would have to ask for his assistance.

Before I could say anything, he stepped forward and effortlessly picked up the crate. "Come on, let's go," he announced, motioning his head towards the cottage.

I nodded and strolled alongside him, unable to resist stealing glances at his appearance. He exuded a casual yet naturally elegant charm, with his slightly tousled dirty blonde hair, a small beard gracing his striking face, and a tall, sturdy frame. I guessed he was probably in his early thirties.

Our eyes met, and warmth rushed to my cheeks. Quickly, I averted my gaze, my fingers instinctively tracing the scar on my cheek. Perhaps he noticed my discomfort, for he too lowered his eyes. In silence, we continued our stroll, each lost in our own thoughts.

Once inside the cottage, Frenchie helped me in putting away the groceries, even though I did not ask him to. When we finished, I waited for him to leave, but instead, he paused to look around and my cheeks turned pink with embarrassment because the cottage looked messy, with my clothes scattered everywhere.

"Thank you, Frenchie. I appreciate the help with the groceries," I said, putting on a smile while subtly pointing my head towards the door.

He caught the hint and nodded, his boots making a soft thudding sound as he walked toward the exit. But then he stopped, pivoting on his heels to face me. The air between us turned electric as our eyes locked. "You really ought to leave here. This isn't a place for someone like you."

I felt my face flush hot, my heart pounding in indignation. "Someone like me? What's that supposed to mean?" I shot back.

He folded his arms, filling the doorway with his broad frame. "A lone woman, in an abandoned estate. Why in God's name would you pick this job?"

"Who I am or why I'm here is none of your business," I countered, eyes narrowing.

His mouth twisted into a smirk. "What about screaming your lungs out earlier?"

I clenched my fists, teeth gritting so hard I could hear it. "That was—"

He took a step closer, his eyes falling to my lips, making me nervous. "You really don't get it, do you? There's evil here. Darkness that you can't even begin to comprehend. That's why people steer clear of this place."

But I refused to back down. "Then what are you doing here?"

"I've got a place in the nearby village. I come in the morning and leave by dusk. And let me tell you, even that's too long." his eyes finally moving from my lips to my eyes.

"Why? Because of this 'darkness'?" I asked.

He let out an exasperated sigh. "Yes, because of the darkness. Did you know there was a maid named Chloe who was brutally murdered here by her husband, Ichabod? Then there was Martha, a grieving mother who took her own life after her child succumbed to a terrible sickness." His words were delivered with emphasis. He raised his voice, his face contorted with frustration, as he stepped closer to me and I involuntarily backed away. "The last tenant of the manor, a man named Martin, lost his sanity and killed a thief before turning the weapon on himself. And most recently, a priest was summoned to bless this place, only to meet his own gruesome end by hanging himself within these very walls." His eyes bore into mine, as though to convey the weight of the horrifying stories. "So let me tell you Evelynn. The darkness of this place is very real. Think about your family, your friends. Do you want to put them through the agony of losing you to this godforsaken place?"

His words left me feeling shocked. Lady Cassandra had failed to mention these chilling details when she spoke to me about the history of the manor.

I wasn't sure if he was trying to scare me or if those stories were real. Although I had firsthand seen a figure chasing me, I had encountered ghosts before and knew I could handle it. There are things in life people must bear, whether they like it or not.

I wasn't about to be intimidated. This job meant too much to me. I wasn't planning on staying here for a lifetime, just a few months to save enough money to find Ava. So, I responded firmly, "I didn't come here for a lecture. You're the groundskeeper, not my guardian."

The tension in the room was so thick, you could cut it with a knife. He glared at me, his nostrils flaring. "Fine. But don't say I didn't warn you."

"I didn't ask for your warning. Kindly get out of here, Sir. Right now." I retorted, my voice channeling my bitterness.

He scowled at me one last time, and then stormed out.

My anger felt as though it was at the boiling point as I stood in the doorway, but then something caught my eye. A pigeon, flying full toward the manor, slammed into a window and tumbled to the ground below.

A pang of sorrow hit me and I forgot all about my anger. I couldn't just stand there; I had to do something. Sprinting toward the fallen bird, I brushed past Frenchie who was in the midst of walking. My eyes welled up as I gently lifted the injured pigeon into my hands.

Frenchie, now curious, came to where I was. He watched me intently as I softly stroked the pigeon's feathers, his eyes studying me as closely.

My tears fell onto the pigeon's soft plumage as I

whispered soothing words, "Oh, little one, you'll be okay."

Frenchie touched my tear-streaked cheek, and for a brief moment, his gesture caught me off guard. I blinked in surprise. He then cleared his throat and gently took the bird from my trembling hand and began to rub the pigeon's wings with care.

"Seems like the wing bone is out of place. It can be fixed. Don't worry Evelynn." he said with concern, as he kept working his finger on the pigeon's wing.

I watched in wonder as the bird's eyes slowly blinked open, and it started to regain its strength. After a few experimental flaps, the pigeon hopped and then took flight.

I turned to Frenchie. "Will it be alright?"

Frenchie met my gaze with a glint in his eyes. "Of course."

Curious, he finally asked, "Why did you shed tears for a pigeon?"

I replied earnestly, "Because it could feel. Anything that can feel pain, I feel for it."

His expression softened, and then he quietly walked away, leaving me by the manor.

Chapter 9

DESPITE MY LINGERING fear from the strange events and Frenchie's warning, I didn't let it stop me from doing my job. I had been on the estate for over a week, and so far, I had only managed to clean a small part of the ground floor. It was about time I gathered my courage and went further into the manor.

I opened the curtains wide to let in as much daylight as possible and turned on all the gas lamps. With more light around, the manor felt less scary. Taking a deep breath, I gathered my cleaning supplies and went from one room to the other. I did my best to put aside my fear and focus on my work. As the hours passed, Blackwood Manor slowly started to look less intimidating.

I threw myself into my work, determined to make the manor a cleaner and more pleasant place. I dusted off antique furniture, and polished away years of neglect. The soft light filtering through the curtains kept the shadows at bay, and I felt less afraid as I immersed myself in the tasks at hand. But then, as I reached the master bedroom, and leaned over to straighten the bedsheet, I felt a chilling sensation, like icy fingers were brushing against my exposed neck. Goosebumps popped up on my skin, and I froze, the room suddenly growing colder. My heart raced as I slowly turned, a sense of dread washing over me.

No one was there.

Empty. The room was empty.

Taking a deep breath, I closed my eyes and counted to ten, each number pushing the fear further away. My heart slowed down, falling back to its regular rhythm.

I've got a job to do and I'm a witch. I can handle this.

Opening my eyes, I clenched my fists and fixed my gaze ahead. "Enough! Leave. Me. Be! I command you to leave me be!" My voice grew louder with each word, echoing off the walls. I felt the room respond, as if it were a living thing. It quivered, then settled. Silence washed over the room, and I knew I'd won this round. Wearing a satisfied grin, I got back to my chores.

Once my work for the day was done, I was on my way out when a door in the hallway creaked open. I halted my steps. My brain told me to get out of the manor but the scent of old papers forced me to peek inside, and when I did, I found it was a library. Not just any library, but a massive one, with towering bookshelves that stretched up to a high, vaulted ceiling. The books were bathed in a soft light. However, the amount of dust was overwhelming. Feeling a strong urge to tidy up, I began to dust the library. After a while, once it started looking a bit better, I paused to take in my surroundings. My fingertips gently skimmed along the rows of worn book spines, each one a gateway to stories from another time.

My eyes were drawn to a particular leather-bound diary, its surface aged but well-crafted, stamped with the name "Fredrick".

Maybe this belonged to the owner of the manor. Lady Cassandra had mentioned his name was Fredrick Blackwood.

I considered picking it up, but another rather peculiar set of books caught my attention. It was a collection of romance stories.

Oh, how I'd yearned for such books when I was a young girl! My mother had never allowed me to have them, though. Eagerly, I picked up a few of the volumes and settled into a chair, becoming completely engrossed.

As I read tales of handsome princes and damsels in distress, for a while I forgot all about the haunting mysteries of the grand manor and simply enjoyed being lost in those captivating books.

I must have dozed off while reading because when I woke up, it was quite a shock. I found myself sitting in a chair in a vast room filled with the glow of countless candles. Heavy red velvet curtains hung around, casting strange and unsettling shadows on the walls. I stood up and went to the window, pulling back the curtain and I saw it was now nighttime. Fear gripped me, and I suddenly remembered Frenchie's warning about not staying in the manor after dark.

I rushed towards the door, desperate to leave the room. But then, something threw me onto the bed, and fear overcame me, making me scream. I felt utterly powerless, consumed by panic. And that's when I saw it—a horrifying figure looming over me. The creature possessed striking crimson eyes, and his features resembled those of a human, save for his obsidian skin. When he opened his mouth, revealing a set of jagged teeth, I opened my mouth to scream, but no sound came out.

And then I saw the creature's enormous tongue extend from its mouth, inching dangerously close to my face.

The moment its tongue made contact with my skin, a strong feeling of disgust washed over me. I desperately wished to pull away and free myself, but my body remained still. The sensation of its touch was beyond description, unlike anything I had ever experienced before.

Tears ran down my face as I gazed fearfully into the monster's eyes, feeling as though they could pierce into the depths of my soul. And then, as if in response to my gaze, it stopped licking my face.

The creature cocked its head in a puzzled manner, its blood-red eyes locked onto mine. "You can see me?" It asked, sounding bewildered.

I nodded cautiously in response.

Instantly the creature retreated, and I felt the sudden return of control over my limbs. As I sat up and observed it, I noticed its muscular physique adorned with intricate glowing glyphs. And it was surely male.

The moment our eyes met again, he emitted a furious howl that sent shivers down my body and neared me.

"Despite my desire to consume you, my dark rose," he murmured while twirling a strand of my raven hair between his fingers, "I'll grant you a single opportunity."

With those words, the creature effortlessly raised me into the air, gripping my throat firmly. "Never set foot in this place again, or you'll rue the day!"

He increased the pressure around my neck and asked, "Got it?" I nodded in response.

With a sudden jerk, he threw me, and I tumbled to the floor. I scrambled to my feet, my heart pounding, desperately searching for a way out, my body trembling.

The creature scaled the wall like a lizard. From the corner of the ceiling, he screeched, revealing his fangs and tongue, which filled me with fear.

I rushed out of the room as fast as my trembling legs could carry me, desperate to escape the horrors that had unfolded within those cursed walls. In my frantic haste, I bolted through the main door, but my reckless flight was abruptly halted when I tripped over an uneven rock just outside the manor. With a painful thud, I crashed to the ground, a sharp cry escaping my lips.

Holding onto my aching ankle, I tried to catch my breath and calm my racing heart. In my moment of vulnerability, I couldn't resist taking a quick look back at the manor's windows. And there they were—the tormented souls that had been trapped within those cursed walls, their faces filled with unending sorrow and unfulfilled wishes.

It was a heart-wrenching scene—a woman, cradling a child, with a mournful gaze; a man and a woman dressed as servants standing side by side, their expressions filled with deep sadness; and two men with clothing stained in what seemed like blood, their eyes empty and unsettling.

As the first rays of sunlight touched the ground, those spectral faces disappeared from the window, leaving me with a chilling realization—I had spent the entire night inside the manor. With my ankle throbbing in pain, I struggled to stand, feeling vulnerable and helpless.

Suddenly, two strong arms reached out and grabbed me. I looked up and saw it was Frenchie. His face showed concern, and his eyes were filled with worry. He carefully helped me stand and I leaned against him.

"You're injured. Let me carry you," he said gently, his voice reassuring.

"Carry me?" I asked, feeling uncertain. Being fully aware of my fuller figure, I doubted whether he could lift me. Attempting to protest, I added, "No, it's fine. I'm quite…"

But before I could finish my sentence, he swiftly picked me up in a bridal style.

"Heavy? Yes, but I can handle it," he declared with a soft smile, his strong arms supporting me effortlessly.

Frenchie carried me back to the cottage, his steps

measured and steady. He gently laid me on the bed, his touch tender and comforting, yet his face betrayed his underlying anger and worry.

In a stern tone, he scolded me, "I explicitly warned you not to go into that place at night."

"I... I lost track of time," I stammered, my voice shaking.

Frenchie's frustration was visible as he retorted, "Lost track of time? That's your excuse? Do you realize how dangerous it could have been? I gave you a clear warning. How could you act so recklessly?"

"Recklessly?" I shouted, my own frustration in my voice. "Please, mind your tone. I didn't know there would be an actual monstrous creature inside that manor! I can handle ghosts and hauntings, but facing a real-life monster? I was terrified, Frenchie. It felt like it was going to kill me. I'm still so scared. What if it follows me here?"

Tears welled up in my eyes, and I couldn't hold back my sobs. Frenchie's stern facade melted away, replaced by a look of regret as he let out a heavy sigh. He reached out, his hand gently resting on my shoulder, and offered an apology, "I'm truly sorry for my words, Evelynn. I didn't mean to be so harsh. Please forgive me. I'll stay with you so you don't have to worry. Are you hurt anywhere else?" I shook my head, wiping my tears.

Frenchie sat on the edge of the bed and gently lifted my foot, placing it in his lap to examine it and I looked at him shocked. "Your ankle should get better in a day or two. It seems like a minor twist," he reassured me. However, I found it hard to focus on his words. My eyes were drawn to the window beside my bed, offering a view of the Blackwood manor outside.

"The souls," I whispered, my voice heavy with sorrow and helplessness.

Frenchie's gaze sharpened. "You can see them, can't you?"

It wasn't a secret I often shared, but in this moment, I felt compelled to reveal my unique ability. I nodded slowly. "Yes, I can see them. It's been like that since I was a child. But let me assure you, I don't dabble in witchcraft or anything like that."

Frenchie's expression softened, "I'm not concerned about witchcraft. My heart goes out to you, knowing that you can see the pain and suffering of these spirits, and you can't share it with anyone else. And about the souls of the manor, Evelynn, you may be the first to see them. Others might have sensed their haunting, but you've witnessed their presence firsthand."

I held my head, a headache beginning to form. "They're trapped. I wish there was something I could do to help them, to set them free."

"I understand your empathy, Evelynn. But unfortunately, there's nothing you can do for them. Right now, you need to focus on yourself and your own well-being." He gently squeezed my foot in his lap,"No need to be a saint and put others before yourself."

His words ignited an anger inside me.

"Helping someone doesn't mean I want to be a saint!" I snapped back, my frustration clear in my voice. I stared at him, waiting for him to get it.

A smile tugged at his lips, and he shook his head. "I didn't mean to upset you."

"Well, you do say things and then apologize for it a lot. Maybe you should think before speaking," I retorted. His chuckle in response only added to my irritation.

Clearly, he found my anger amusing.

"Did anyone ever tell you that you look lovely when you're angry," his comment caught me off guard and I blinked at him, surprised and at a loss for words. "You know, if you keep making that face, I might have to do something about it."

How dare he?!

I raised my hand to slap him. But before I could do anything, he gently grabbed my hand and brought it to his lips. He kissed the back of my hand, and I felt unable to move.

Frenchie's other hand went to my face, tracing my lips and then moving down to my chin. My stomach was in knots, his touch felt electric. I knew I shouldn't want this, but it had been so long. Before I could say anything, he gently lifted my chin and pulled me in for a kiss. The moment our lips touched, my mind went blank and I froze in place. Seconds later, when he pulled away, his lips hovered inches from my ear, his warm breath against my skin.

He backed away to look at my face, but I couldn't meet his eyes. "Frenchie, I... I think you should go. It's daytime now, and I think I'll be fine," I stammered, my breaths labored, overwhelmed by what had just happened.

He looked down, nodded, and got off the bed. He gently touched my head, and I closed my eyes but didn't meet his gaze. Then, he silently left the cottage.

Chapter 10

A S I WRAPPED A cloth tightly around my throbbing ankle, the memory of the kiss kept coming back to me. Heat surged up my cheeks, a delicious shame that made the room feel ten degrees warmer. Those lips, that tingling sensation—it had left me light-headed, gasping for air like I'd been underwater for too long.

Get yourself together, Evelynn!

I shook my head, snapping out of my reverie and flung open the heavy curtains, letting the waning late afternoon light wash over the room. And there he was, Frenchie. Standing outside. My heart started to beat faster. I yanked the curtains shut and took a shallow breath, confused by my own reaction.

I couldn't let my emotions disrupt my work any longer. The chores needed to be done, and I was determined not to be distracted. I went to the kitchen, my thoughts still in turmoil.

I decided to make myself a calming cup of tea and picked up the kettle to put water in it. But before I could even turn on the tap, a sudden touch on my shoulder sent shock coursing through me. The kettle slipped from my grasp, clattering noisily on the floor.

My heart raced as I swiftly turned around, my eyes wide with astonishment. There, in the cottage with me, stood Frenchie. It was as if he had appeared out of thin air, his presence both unexpected and perplexing. "How did you manage to get in here?" I stammered, my words trembling as they escaped my lips.

He pointed to the open door, his face expressionless.

"No, I mean, why just barge in?" I asked, a bit flustered but trying to control my emotions.

His eyes twinkled mischievously. "I saw you peeking through the window. I thought you might need company."

Damn, he'd caught me. My face flushed a shade of red that could probably rival a ripe tomato.

Changing topics, I asked, "Have you been outside this whole time?" He simply nodded. "Would you like some tea?"

He said, "Yes," but as I reached for the kettle again, he guided me to a chair with a gentle touch. "Let me make it for you. You shouldn't be on your feet too much."

I sat, silently watching him navigate my kitchen, impressed by his familiarity. He was eye-catching, no doubt about it. My eyes traced the strong contours of his back, shoulders, arms—and damn it, he'd caught me again! A smirk curled the edge of his mouth, and I bit my lip, looking away.

When the tea was ready, he handed me a cup. "Not having any?" I asked, taking a sip.

"No. But go ahead, enjoy yours," he responded with a shrug as he sat across from me.

After an awkward silence, Frenchie cleared his throat, "About what happened," he said and I closed my eyes. I knew where this was headed.

"I was out of line," Frenchie said, sincerity in his

words. "I'm sorry, Evelynn."

"Let's not talk about it," I answered, brushing the topic aside.

He nodded, his gaze sweeping over the quaint cottage before settling on me once more. "Evelynn," he began, "could we perhaps be friends?"

My heart lightened a bit. "I'd appreciate that," I confessed. "I could definitely use a friend in this place."

He chuckled, his eyes glancing toward the window where the sun was setting. "I should get going," he announced, walking to the door.

"Alright. I suppose I'll see you tomorrow." I replied.

The door closed behind him but once he was gone my thoughts were occupied by nothing but Frenchie.

Chapter 11

FTER THAT DAY, Frenchie made daily visits to check on me. We would have tea, chat, and it became a comforting routine that made being at Blackwood Manor more tolerable.

As time passed, our interactions grew more comfortable. One day, as he examined my healing foot, his touch deepened into a massage, his skilled fingers tracing soothing patterns across my swollen ankle.

He must have noticed the surprise in my eyes because he quickly explained, "I'm just examining your feet and I must say, they are quite lovely," all the while working his fingers on my foot.

A moan escaped my lips as he ran his finger

along the sole of my foot, and I quickly placed a hand over my mouth in embarrassment.

Frenchie chuckled softly, his touch never faltering. "You don't have to be flustered, you know. It's just a foot massage."

I could feel my ears burn with embarrassment but I couldn't deny the pleasure that coursed through my body. "I know, but it feels... nicer than I expected."

A mischievous glint danced in his eyes. "I can make you feel even nicer," He purred, his voice low and husky.

Before I could respond, his gaze was locked onto mine and he had brought my foot to his lips, his warm breath teasing my skin. My eyes widened in shock, watching as he expertly traced kisses along the arch of my foot. A wave of pleasure washed over me, igniting a fire in my core. And when he sucked each toe, I squirmed.

"What are you doing, Frenchie!" I giggled, my body trembling with excitement.

"Worshiping your beautiful feet," he said, his eyes never leaving mine as he slowly took my foot into his mouth, his tongue skillfully stroking and caressing my skin. I was lost in the sensation, my mind and body completely ensnared by his sensual touch.

With a flick of his eyes, he moved to my other foot, giving the same attention and causing me to moan again with pleasure. The intensity of the moment was almost overwhelming.

When he finally released my foot, I was left breathless and wanting more. Frenchie's gaze locked with mine, the fire in his eyes matching the burning desire in my own.

"That was... amazing," I managed to whisper, my heart racing.

A sly smile tugged at the corners of his lips. "I aim to please."

With our eyes locked, I leaned in without thinking and kissed him. Our lips met in a sweet, electric connection, and when we finally broke the kiss, his mouth hung agape, his eyes fixated on my lips.

"You're perfect, Evelynn," he breathed and his words made my heart skip a beat.

The day finally arrived when my foot had healed

enough for Frenchie to take me on a walk. The autumn air was crisp, signaling the end of September, and I wrapped a shawl around my shoulders as we left the cottage.

"I don't like the energy here," he said, avoiding eye contact and instead gazing at the manor's garden.

The garden did look forgotten. Broken statues lay strewn about, and it was as if the vines and thorns had claimed the place for their own. It was easy to see why Frenchie felt the way he did.

As we stepped into the woods, it was like crossing into another world. The air felt lighter, purer somehow. Trees heavy with ripe fruit reached up to the sky, while strawberry vines snaked along the ground, offering their sweet bounty.

Frenchie plucked an apple from a nearby tree and handed it to me with a smile. "Try this," he said. I took a bite, and its sweetness exploded in my mouth.

"It's delicious," I remarked, taking another bite. As I did, my thoughts wandered back to our earlier times together. I remembered how Frenchie had teased me, how he'd playfully nibbled on my feet, and those few sweet kisses we'd shared. Yet despite those intimate moments, that was as far as things had gone between us.

Our steps eventually led us to the estate's cemetery and suddenly the atmosphere grew heavier. As we strolled, we came across Fredrick Blackwood's grave first. A sense of gravity settled over us; this was the patriarch, the origin of the estate's current state. But it was the next tombstone that really seemed to catch Frenchie's attention. We had stopped at a grave marked 'Peter Blackwood.'

"Why are we here?" I finally asked, the air heavy and making me uncomfortable.

"I feel drawn here, like I'm supposed to find something—or maybe someone." He said.

As we sat down on the grass near the headstone, I commented, "Peter Blackwood. He must have been related to Fredrick Blackwood."

Frenchie nodded his head, his brow furrowing, "I suppose. But look at dates on the tombstones. The boy must have been so young when he passed away. I can't even comprehend what losing a child does to a parent."

His words broke my heart and even though my

Ava was well and alive, being away from her tormented me. Seeing the glisten of tears in my eyes, Frenchie asked, "Are you a mother? Have you ever been married, Evelynn?"

I met his gaze and nodded, "I was married once. Divorce happened, and now I have a daughter somewhere out there."

"Somewhere out there? What do you mean?" he asked, his voice gentle.

"My husband had me committed to an asylum, then divorced me and took our daughter, Ava. When I left the asylum, I couldn't find her," I confessed, my voice on the brink of breaking.

His reaction was immediate—Frenchie shot up, anger blazing in his eyes. "That scoundrel. If I had been there, I swear he'd be in pieces!"

"I wish," I whispered, adding, "I took this job to save money. I plan to find Ava."

Frenchie's eyes softened, filled with empathy. "I'm so sorry, Evelynn. I hope you find your daughter."

At that moment, the flood gate opened and tears ran down my face; Frenchie embraced me as if to offer me solace. "I miss her every damn day," I managed to choke out.

"I can understand. One day you will be reunited with your daughter. I'm sure of it," he whispered, holding me close. Then, he gently wiped away my tears with his lips and kissed me. For that brief moment, I felt that things would get better.

Chapter 12

ANOTHER WEEK PASSED without me setting foot inside the manor. I was avoiding it like the plague, and I also worried that Lady Cassandra would discover my neglect of my duties. I intended to enter the manor with Frenchie, but I hadn't gotten around to asking him yet. I planned to bring it up the following morning, but that very night, a storm rolled in.

It felt like the heavens had opened up and the rain was relentless. Soon, it wasn't just the sound of raindrops pelting the roof; a puddle began to spread across the floor of the cottage forming a tiny lake. The ceiling was betraying its age, droplets seeping through cracks. If this downpour didn't let up, I had a sinking feeling that the entire roof could cave in.

Ignoring Frenchie's earlier warnings, I had no choice but to head for the manor. Cold bit me, my clothes sticking like a second skin as I left the cottage and walked towards the manor. As I got closer, a bolt of lightning cracked across the sky, casting shadows over the Blackwood manor. Just as I reached for my set of keys, with shaky hands, the heavy door creaked open on its own, as if inviting me in.

Stepping inside, my eyes widened at the scene that greeted me. The place was aglow with candles and lanterns casting a warm and inviting light throughout the grand hallway. It felt as though I had stumbled upon a lavish celebration right there in the manor.

The room was filled with people, elegantly dressed in their finest attire. The women wore silk gowns, and the men were impeccably dressed in suits that spoke of sophistication. Yet what truly captured my attention were the masks. Everyone wore one, concealing their faces behind an air of mystery.

Entering the room felt like stepping back in time into an extravagant party, alive with music and graceful dancing. Masked guests glided effortlessly across the floor, their every move perfectly timed to the rhythm of the music.

I stood amidst this spectacle, wet and disoriented, feeling entirely out of place. Strangely, no one seemed to notice my presence; it was as if I were a ghost.

Drawn to a grand mirror hanging on the wall, I saw my own reflection but the celebration happening behind was not there. All I saw in the mirror was myself standing in the dark manor all alone.

In that same mirror, a woman appeared behind me and I recognized her. She was the beautiful woman from the paintings. She seemed to be fixated on adjusting her mask, completely oblivious to my presence. Once satisfied, she went to her dance partner, and their chemistry was undeniable. It was as if they were lost in their own world.

The man eventually guided her toward a grand staircase, and she followed without hesitation. I trailed behind, driven by a curiosity I couldn't ignore.

They reached a moonlit balcony, and there, I

found myself a spectator to a passionate kiss. It was a captivating scene, pulling me into its emotional intensity even as I remained a mere observer.

The woman broke the kiss, her chest heaving with desire as she whispered with intensity, "Ben, I love you."

Ben, the object of her affection, responded with equal fervor, his voice filled with emotion, "And I love you, Elizabeth."

As I stood there, an accidental observer to their most intimate moment, I watched as the woman, Elizabeth, her eyes sparkling with joy, shared a revelation that sent ripples through the room. "Ben," she breathed, her voice barely above a whisper, "I'm pregnant."

Ben's face lit up with a radiant smile, and he seemed unable to resist the impulse to pull her close for another passionate kiss. "That's wonderful, Elizabeth," he exclaimed, his joy echoing hers. "I don't care if the child is mine or his; I'll love you and the child with all my heart. I can't bear to see you with him any longer."

Elizabeth's eyes shone with happiness as she returned his kiss, her voice quivering with emotion.

"Just a little more time, Ben, and everything will be alright."

As the moon cast its silvery glow upon the balcony, a sudden shift in the atmosphere brought a sense of tension to the lovers' embrace. Ben, his senses sharp, broke the kiss with Elizabeth and cast an alert gaze towards the direction of the approaching footsteps.

"He's coming." Ben said.

With a final lingering kiss, Ben gently disentangled himself from Elizabeth's arms, his movements swift and determined.

Elizabeth watched him as he deftly climbed over the balcony railing and onto the balcony's edge. His every movement was calculated to avoid making a sound as he disappeared

With a composed demeanor, Elizabeth turned to face the entrance of the balcony. As the man entered, my breath caught in my throat. It was... Frenchie! He was dressed in attire that seemed straight out of a bygone era, a stark contrast to the Frenchie I knew. My Frenchie had always been kind and playful. This man, however, exuded an air of authority and cruelty. His eyes watched

Elizabeth as she stood on the moonlit balcony.

"What are you doing here, my love? The guests eagerly await your return," he inquired, his voice laced with venom.

"I...I just needed some fresh air, Fredrick. I'll be down in a minute." Elizabeth stammered.

However, Frenchie, or should I say Fredrick, moved closer, his fingers gently tracing the contours of Elizabeth's lips. "Your swollen lips tell a different story," he remarked. In a sudden, shocking gesture, he delivered a harsh and stinging slap across her face, causing me to gasp in disbelief.

His fingers tightened around Elizabeth's throat, cruel and unyielding, as he continued to unleash his wrath. "Don't mistake my resolve, Elizabeth. Your lover has dared to tread on this ground, and if he dares to return, I'll ensure his end! Remember my words."

Fear and panic overwhelmed me as I watched the horrifying scene unfold. Even though I knew they couldn't see me or hear me, I couldn't help but scream.

In that moment, Frenchie's gaze locked onto

mine, and to my disbelief, he could see me! Elizabeth's head turned in my direction, and even she could see me as her eyes widened in shock and terror.

"I warned you to stay away!" he thundered, his voice echoing through the night from the balcony. Suddenly, his eyes sunk back into their sockets, the flesh from his face began to rot, and he transformed into a decomposed and horrifying figure.

I turned and dashed out of the balcony, and once again, the manor was shrouded in darkness. Frenchie chased after me as I ran. Fear gripped me, causing my heart to race. I hurried through the dim corridor, the sound of my footsteps echoing in the ancient hallways.

Every door I tried was locked. My trembling hands fumbled with a bunch of keys, desperately trying to find the right one that would open the door so I could hide.

My breaths came in short, shallow gasps as I sprinted, my hands shaking with fear and adrenaline. Finally, I found a door that was unlocked. Without hesitation, I flung it open and darted inside, slamming the door shut behind me.

Inside the room, I pressed against the door, my chest heaving from exhaustion and fear. His warning still echoed in my ears: "Stay away from my manor!"

I knew he was drawing near. Overwhelmed, I fell to my knees and crawled beneath the bed, seeking refuge. I closed my eyes, tears running down my face, my terror threatening to consume me.

I heard an agonizing cry pierce the air.. "Ahh... I can't bear it any longer!" a woman's anguished words echoed through the room. "Get it out of me!"

My eyes widened as I witnessed the surreal transformation of the room. It was as if time itself had rewound, erasing decades of neglect and decay. The room had been restored to its former glory, a dramatic change from the neglected condition it was in just moments before.

"Push, Elizabeth! The baby is on its way. You must push!" A calm but resolute voice, that of a midwife, urged Elizabeth. Hidden from their view, I watched as Elizabeth, tears rolling down her cheeks, followed the midwife's instructions, her expression contorting with intense pain.

The midwife wiped the sweat off from Elizabeth's brow, "Lord Fredrick is just outside. Don't you worry my dear. Just push."

Tension hung in the air as Elizabeth's efforts intensified and she let out a pained scream. I couldn't help but empathize with her. I had gone through this pain. I knew exactly what she was feeling, how much pain she was in.

Finally, with a final, exhausted push, the baby was born— a boy. The midwife wrapped the baby in a cloth and gave him in Elizabeth's arms. The boy had striking blue eyes and a crown of blonde hair, unmistakably resembling both Elizabeth and Fredrick. However, Elizabeth's expression held no joy or relief. Instead, it was filled with disdain. It was clear the child was not a result of her forbidden affair with Ben.

With trembling hands, she handed the newborn to the midwife, her face filled with a mixture of despair and resentment. But the ordeal was not over, as a surge of pain gripped her once more and she screamed.

In a shocking turn of events, Elizabeth gave birth to a second child, this one bearing dark hair and eyes that mirrored her lover's. The midwife urgently called for Fredrick to join them, and when he entered the room and laid eyes on the dark-haired baby, his face contorted with fury. The truth was now painfully apparent.

"How... how is this even possible?" Frenchie's voice quivered with disbelief and anger. "One child of mine, and the other... not mine. Is it even possible?"

"I.. I.. have never seen anything like this, my lord," the midwife said, her voice shaking with trepidation.

Fury surged through Fredrick, contorting his face as he gripped Elizabeth's shoulders and shook her violently. "You wish to mock me, don't you? To make a fool of me, a man who can't even keep his own wife? To suggest that my wife needs another man!"

A bitter, mirthless laugh escaped Elizabeth's lips. "I suppose so. I despise you, Fredrick."

Fredrick's hand rose, poised to strike Elizabeth, but the midwife's voice intervened. "Something is wrong with the baby."

Startled, Fredrick released his grip on Elizabeth

and ran to the dark-haired baby, snatching him from the midwife's arms. Panic and desperation were on his face as he rubbed the baby's back and chest vigorously.

"Come on, little one," Fredrick urged, his voice filled with worry. It was clear that, even though the child was not his own, he was deeply concerned for its well-being.

Fredrick attempted to provide the infant with life-giving breaths, pressing his mouth to the tiny one. Meanwhile, Elizabeth's screams echoed through the room, her agony echoing like a mournful wail.

"Your hatred has killed him! Your hatred, Fredrick!" Elizabeth's anguished cries pierced the air as the midwife struggled to restrain her. The room became a haunting scene of sorrow and despair.

The grim realization hit them hard—there was no life left in the baby. Frenchie gently placed the lifeless infant into a crib and sank to his knees looking defeated. Meanwhile, Elizabeth, still bleeding from childbirth, managed to pull herself out of bed. Tears streamed down her face as she approached Fredrick, her anger and grief driving her to grab his hair and strike him repeatedly.

"I hate you. I'll always hate you, Fredrick!" She cried out, her voice quivering with devastation. Then, in a sudden and unexplainable twist, she turned her attention towards me. It was as if a curtain had been lifted, and for the first time, everyone in the room, including Fredrick and the midwife, could see me.

Fear seized me, and I made a mad dash to escape, my feet pounding on the cold, stone floor. But a presence chased me, and when I dared to glance back, it wasn't Fredrick but the same nightmarish black creature I had seen in the manor before.

It was an abyss of darkness, with blood-red eyes that gleamed with malice and teeth like jagged razors. Its body was adorned with glowing golden symbols that cast eerie shadows in the dim light.

And then, just as I thought my end was near, it seized me with a grip that felt like icy death, its clawed hands wrapping around my throat, crushing the air from my lungs. I gasped for breath, my vision darkening at the edges, and begged for mercy.

"Please," I stammered, my voice trembling with

fear, "Spare me!"

The creature's reply was a chilling whisper, its words dripping with malevolence. "You dare trespass in this realm," it hissed, "and now, you shall pay the price."

As terror surged through me, the creature's grip tightened further, its claws digging into the flesh on my chest. Pain shot through my body, and I cried out in agony.

The monster gazed at me with its fiery red eyes, and for a moment, those intense eyes softened. It reached out and wiped away a tear from my cheek, then tasted it with its tongue. In that instant, its eyes lost their fiery redness and I could see Frenchie's azure eyes.

"Frenchie?" The moment his name escaped my lips, I saw a flash of recognition in his eyes. But as quickly as it came, it disappeared , the anger came back, transforming him once more into a terrifying creature before me.

His grip on me suddenly tightened, crushing me before he hurled me across the room. I slammed into the wall with a painful thud, feeling the wind rush out of my lungs. As I scrambled back to my feet, I tasted the bitter tang of blood in my mouth. I looked at the creature, his face a twisted version of the man I knew as Frenchie.

My eyes darted around the room, landing on a candle stand. Seizing the moment, I grabbed it and hurled it toward him. The candles missed, but the curtain behind him caught fire. I took my chance and bolted for the door, legs propelling me forward as if my life depended on it—because it did.

Behind me, an ear-piercing howl rattled the room's walls. The creature lunged at the growing fire, perhaps aiming to extinguish it. I didn't wait to find out, and burst out the door and into the night.

Rain slapped my face as I ran across the open grounds. I veered into the woods, my feet slipping in the mud, my breath ragged. Every step I took, he mirrored, closing the gap between us.

Then I felt a tug—my dress ripping from behind, exposing my skin to the cold rain. I kept running, but I was tiring out. A trip, a fall, and I was on my stomach. A weight landed on my back, flipping me over to face him.

"You made me angry," he snarled, his eyes filled with fury."But the chase was fun. Ready for your punishment?"

Desperately, I tried to push him away, but he was too strong. Tears stung my eyes as he forced his tongue into my mouth. I struggled to speak, to tell him to leave me alone, but I couldn't. He flipped me over onto my stomach and pinned me down with his full body weight. I couldn't move, couldn't see what he was doing. All I could see was the line of trees in front of me.

"I warned you about the manor, my dark rose, didn't I? Yet you couldn't resist," he murmured, his voice tinged with a darkness that made my spine tingle. "Now, in these haunted woods, the hunt is over. Feeling scared? You really should, because tonight, you're not just my prey—you're my dark craving. You're the desire that haunts my very soul." he growled, twisting his hand in my hair and raising my face from the ground.

I felt a knot in my stomach from pure fear. I knew what was about to happen, and it terrified me, absolutely terrified me. I thrashed and tried kicking out in any and every direction that I could. But when his nails scratched my upper thighs and he tore my knickers, it was then that I realized there was no point in struggling. There was no way I could stop him from taking what he wanted from me. Defeated, I sobbed and stopped moving and lay still on my stomach, accepting the grim reality.

He felt me go still and chuckled, bringing his face close to my ear, he whispered. "So you're ready for this, huh? You want it. Don't you?"

I couldn't believe his audacity. Rage surged within me.

"You're fucked up in the head if you think that," I snapped back as my voice shook with desperation and anger. "I know it's you, Frenchie, and I swear I'll despise you for this, for the rest of my life. I'll always hate you for doing this to me. You're a monster, a devil! May you burn for what you're doing."

Then, a feral roar burst from his lips, so chilling it froze my soul. I braced for the pain, for the finality of it all—but it never came. Trembling, I dared not lift my head, until I heard a haunting howl fill the air and felt the weight keeping me down go away. I scrambled to my knees, turned around, and saw the monster clawing the ground in visible agony. With cautious movements, I sat up, my eyes wide in disbelief and wonder.

"Go away! Run, I beg of you!" he cried out, his voice dripping with desperation. "I'm losing control. Please, just leave. Run!"

Without thinking twice, I shot up and sprinted to my cottage, the monster's screams and howls echoing in the rain. As I burst through the cottage door, I slammed it shut and locked it.

Leaning heavily against the door, I tried to calm my racing heart. My skin tingled where the monster had touched me. Then I felt wetness on my chest— a scratch from the monster, oozing blood. I pressed my back to the door, rocking slowly, a feeble attempt to dispel my terror.

I remained there, suspended in a state of dread, until the chirping of birds signaled dawn. Just as I started to feel a sliver of relief, a hand gently touched mine. I glanced and saw it was Frenchie, crouching next to me. Panic surged, and I tried to scramble away, crawling on my hands and knees. But Frenchie was quick. He moved in front of me, blocking my escape, then reached around to hold me from behind, his grip firmly on my wrists. I was trapped, his strong arms keeping me in place against the cold floor.

"Evelynn. I can explain," Frenchie's voice quivered, desperate.

"Explain? What's there to explain?" I gasped. "You—you fooled me, Frenchie, you've hurt me. You.. you tried to rape me!" I managed to say, each word choked out between sobs.

"No. No. No," he groveled, his voice quivering with sorrow. After releasing his grip on me, he came in front of me. His eyes widened with desperation, and he clenched his fists, pulling at his hair in anguish. "I couldn't control myself. Please, Evelynn, you have to understand. Please. It was tearing me apart, and I had to summon every ounce of strength just to pull away from you."

"Pull yourself away? Look at me, Frenchie! Look at my clothes!" I scoffed as I gestured at my torn and blood-stained gown. "Look what you've done!" My voice trembled with emotion. "If you'd had your way, I would be dead!"

Frenchie looked shattered, his eyes welling up. "I would never intentionally hurt you, you have to know that. From the moment you walked into the manor, I have loved you. Since the moment I removed that stray strand from your face, I have desired you. From the moment your eyes locked with mine, and I felt seen for the first time in many years, my dead heart only wanted you. All I want, all I need is you. Please, I love you, Evelynn."

"Love me? Is this what you call love?" My voice broke as I ripped my nightgown's neckline, exposing the claw marks on my neck and chest.

Frenchie shook his head as if telling himself he didn't do it. He moved toward me, but I held up my hand. "Don't. Don't touch me."

His voice cracked as he spoke, anguish in every word. "I'm so sorry, Evelynn. I died a century ago, and since then, I've been tied to the manor, trapped in its walls. The manor, this cursed estate... It changes me. Morphs me into something dark, uncontrollable. I don't know what I am at night, that's why I never wanted you to come to the manor at night."

"I don't care! I don't know what you are. A ghost, a monster. I just want nothing to do with you."

"Don't say that, I love you, Evelynn," he raised his voice.

"I hate you. I despise you," I cut him off, each word dripping with a bitterness I couldn't contain. "I see you for what you truly are. A monster, both in life and in death.

Anger flashed across his face, and he held me firmly by my shoulders and brought his face so close to mine. "Say you don't mean it! Say it!"

Ignoring the desperation in his voice, I mustered all the strength I had left and pushed him away. "I command you to leave me be." And with those words, a whoosh of wind sucked him out of the cottage, banishing him to wherever he had come from.

As I sank to my knees, my body trembling, I wondered how many more secrets were hidden within the walls of the manor.

Chapter 13

NOT LONG AFTER Frenchie vanished, the gravity of it all hit me like a ton of bricks. I knew I had to run, to put miles between me and the twisted tales of that manor. More than the mysteries or the could-have-beens with Frenchie, my own sanity was on the line.

I packed my things, left the cottage, and started walking away from the estate. I hoped that each step would take me further from the place. But something strange was happening.

No matter how far I walked, everything stayed the same. The same trees, the same landmarks, like I was stuck in a never-ending loop, a never-ending bad dream. Panic began to creep in because it seemed I couldn't just walk away from this nightmare.

The sun was blazing hot, and I was getting really thirsty. I was running out of water fast, and I felt weaker with every step. Eventually, I collapsed under the hot sun, and everything went dark.

When I got up, I could see that I was still inside the estate's boundaries. It was like the place was playing tricks on me, and I couldn't understand why.

I tried to keep going, not giving up but no matter how far I'd go, I'd return to the same spot where I had started. It was like the manor had control over me, and I was just a pawn in its twisted game.

As the sun set, I gave up, tired and defeated. Tears ran down my face. I was stuck, and there seemed to be no way to escape this terrible nightmare. With no other options, I reluctantly returned to the cottage.

I lay on the bed, gazing at the stars through the broken roof, lost in my thoughts. Suddenly, I heard voices coming from the manor's garden. Curiosity got the best of me and I went outside to check. To my surprise, I saw two familiar figures locked in a passionate embrace: Elizabeth and Ben.

"You are the most enchanting woman," Ben said softly, his voice filled with admiration.

Elizabeth smiled as she replied, "And you, my dearest, are the most captivating man."

Their intimate moment paused as they turned their attention to me. I felt frozen in place as Elizabeth approached me, extending her hand to me.

"Don't be afraid, Evelynn," Elizabeth whispered, her voice gentle as the night's breeze. She drew closer and planted a soft kiss on my cheek. In the moonlight, her beauty was undeniable—with her long, golden hair and captivating eyes, she was enchanting. Elizabeth was a sight to behold, leaving me completely enthralled.

Ben approached me, his eyes fixed on mine. With his square jaw and dark features, he exuded an undeniable charm. His dark hair and eyes added to his striking appearance. As he gently trailed his fingers along my arm, a shiver ran down me, and goosebumps rose on my skin.

I took a step back, a mixture of surprise and disbelief coursing through me. "You both, you are

Ben and Elizabeth." I questioned, instinctively putting some distance between myself and Ben. Elizabeth's eyes widened, and she wore a knowing smirk on her face.

"Because you are a soul seer. I could sense that about you," Elizabeth said with curiosity as she gently took my hand and led me to a nearby bench.

"Yes," I answered, my shaky. "In the past, I only saw souls when I was hurting. What's different now? Why can I see you?"

Elizabeth let out a sigh. "Because this place is different, unlike anything else. It's got a dark force hanging over it. The rules from the outside world? They don't apply here."

"The dark force— you mean Frenchie? Or Fredrick? Or the monster, whatever he actually is?" I said, my words came out frustrated.

Elizabeth let out a huff before her expression shifted to one of sorrow, and tears welled up in her eyes. "Yes. That very man. My husband, Fredrick, was a wicked and cruel man. He ruined my life, Evelynn. I was just sixteen when I was forced into a marriage with him. But before him, there was Ben. I, the daughter of a nobleman, and he, a gypsy. Our love story began when we were mere children."

As Ben joined us on the bench, he held Elizabeth by the waist and brought her close to him and then they shared an intimate kiss. "We made a solemn vow to love each other, even beyond the boundaries of death itself, and we have kept that promise," Ben declared, his voice filled with love and sorrow. "Elizabeth's father discovered our love and had me brutally beaten. I was subjected to days of torment, while Elizabeth was wed to Lord Fredrick Blackwood, a man both vile and cruel. His sole obsession was to sire an heir, and he forced himself upon her every night. My Elizabeth was trapped in that nightmarish existence."

"But you found me, my love," Elizabeth said, drawing closer to Ben, as I watched them in fascination. "Ben disguised himself as a servant to work on this estate. This is the very place where we met every night, in the open air, amidst these garden labyrinths, far from prying eyes."

As I sat with them, it was clear to see the deep love that bound Elizabeth and Ben together. Curiosity compelled me to ask, "If you're together, why are you still here?"

Elizabeth's eyes held a haunted look as she explained, "We are tied to this place, unable to leave its grounds. Both the manor and its surroundings are home to a malevolent presence, the monstrous evil that preys upon all who come near— My husband, Fredrick. He made a sinister pact, trading his soul for vengeance when he believed I had betrayed him. Anyone who enters the manor suffers greatly. It's a place steeped in darkness and evil."

As I gazed at the moonlit garden, a nagging question lingered in my mind. "Is there no way to break that tether? To set you two free?" I finally mustered the courage to voice it.

Elizabeth's smile was tender but filled with sadness. "I'm afraid it's not that simple, Evelynn."

Despite her reassurance, a sense of helplessness washed over me. "I wish there was something I could do to help."

Elizabeth's voice was soothing as she urged me, "You're tired, Evelynn. Rest now. We are here, right outside the cottage, to protect you."

Feeling tired and troubled, I went back inside my

cottage. I crawled into bed, seeking the comfort of sleep. Elizabeth's words stayed with me as I closed my eyes, knowing they were nearby, guarding over me from outside the cottage.

Chapter 14

IN JUST A FEW days, I became really close to Elizabeth and Ben. Frenchie was gone, and I didn't miss him. I stayed away from the Blackwood manor and hung out in the garden instead.

One evening, we all sat outside under the moonlight. The glow of the moon seemed to illuminate Elizabeth's skin, and I found myself wondering how beautiful she must have been when she was alive. As for Ben, there was a certain expression in his eyes that gave off a sense of trustworthiness, making me feel genuinely at ease.

I couldn't help but chuckle. "Life is full of surprises. I never thought I'd find friends like you in this place."

Ben nodded in agreement. "Indeed, Evelynn. We're grateful for your presence in our eternal existence."

As the nights passed, we shared stories of our past lives, our dreams, and the tragedies that had brought us together in this place. Our conversations were filled with laughter, camaraderie, and a sense of shared understanding.

I found myself reflecting on my own life. "It's strange how life—or death—can bring people together. I cherish these moments with both of you."

Elizabeth offered her support. "Likewise, Evelynn. You've brought light into our existence."

Ben smiled warmly. "Our bond may have been forged in unusual circumstances, but it's a bond we hold dear."

As we continued to talk, I opened up about my past. "My life before this place was far from peaceful. My husband, Edward, was abusive. He called me a mad woman when I first told him I could see ghosts."

Elizabeth and Ben listened attentively, their expressions filled with sympathy.

"I have a darling daughter named Ava," I continued, tears welling up in my eyes. "But Edward took her away from me, and after our divorce, he committed me to an asylum."

Elizabeth's hand reached out to comfort me. "I'm so sorry, Evelynn."

I nodded, grateful for their understanding. "When I returned home after two long years in that dreadful place, I discovered that Edward had sold our house and vanished with Ava. I've been searching for them ever since."

Ben's eyes held compassion. "You've faced so much hardship, Evelynn." His hand brushed against mine, and he pulled me down onto the soft grass with tenderness. He gazed into my eyes as if he could feel my pain.

"Let us be your refuge, Evelynn. Let us make you forget all the pain and suffering," he whispered, before capturing my lips in a passionate kiss.

Behind me, Elizabeth began to rub my shoulders, her touch sending shivers down my spine. I felt like a putty in their hands, all my worries melting away under their loving touch.

After Ben, it was Elizabeth's turn. She hovered over me, her lips finding mine in a kiss. The warmth of their embrace, the softness of their touch - it was all too much for me.

I couldn't hold back the tears any longer. They ran down my cheeks, a mixture of joy and pain. In this moment, I knew that I was loved. Truly, deeply, and without any boundaries. Their love for me felt as pure and unconditional as the love they felt for each other.

"We love you, Evelynn. We love you like we love each other," Ben said, his fingers gently rubbing my hair.

"Yes, we want you to be with us. We want to give you all the love in the world," Elizabeth added, her voice filled with warmth.

Their words touched me deeply, and the idea of escaping with them, leaving behind all the challenges of this world, was very appealing. But I couldn't give in to that temptation. I still had a reason to keep going—finding my daughter and bringing her home.

I remembered the promise I had made to Ava before she was taken away. I had promised her that

I would keep on living, keep on trying, no matter how hard life got. It was a pledge I intended to keep, a commitment to her that kept me tied to this world, even when I felt so much pain and sadness.

"I can't. I need to keep going for my Ava," was all I could say as tears were still streaming down my face.

Elizabeth and Ben exchanged a meaningful look, and Elizabeth spoke softly, "Then we will stand by your side until your journey reaches its end."

Chapter 15

DAYS HAD PASSED since Ben and Elizabeth made their offer, and their words continued to occupy my thoughts. As I went about my daily tasks around the cottage—carefully avoiding the manor—I couldn't shake the feeling that I was being watched. My eyes darted toward the mansion, and, to my surprise, I saw someone drawing the curtains closed.

I couldn't help but wonder, was it Frenchie behind those curtains? What Elizabeth and Ben had told me about him only deepened my hate for the man. I felt this urge to barge into the manor and confront him, to hold up a mirror to his ugliness.

However, I couldn't bring myself to confront

him, held back by the fear from our last encounter when he had almost raped me in his monstrous form. Instead, I headed to the woods to pick some apples. Although the memory of the previous attack haunted me, making me nervous with every step, I pressed on; I needed those apples.

I reached the apple trees and hesitated, my eyes darting around to make sure I was alone. Gathering my courage, I plucked the first apple from the tree. Just as my hand touched the fruit, a shiver ran through me like a flashback to that terrible night.

I quickly picked a few more, stuffing them into my basket. My hands were shaking, but I pushed through. "You're okay," I whispered to myself, "you're okay."

I left the woods as fast as I could, the basket of apples feeling heavier with each step. That's when I saw the letter from Mrs. Darcy at my doorstep, and for a moment, my fear was replaced by a glimmer of hope. Could it be news about Ava?

I entered the cottage and carefully opened the letter, my emotions running high.

My Dearest Evelynn,

I hope this letter finds you as well as can be

expected. I have news to share, and I fear it won't bring the comfort we had hoped for.

After searching tirelessly, I managed to locate your estranged husband, Edward, in London. My initial hope was that he. might have information about Ava, your beloved daughter. But the truth is heartbreaking.

Ava was with him until a few weeks ago, when she fell ill to smallpox, a cruel and unforgiving disease. Despite all efforts to save her, she passed away peacefully, under the care of medical professionals.

Evelynn, I wish I could offer you better news. Losing a child brings an unimaginable pain, and my heart goes out to you in this difficult time.

Please know that I'm here for you, ready to support you in any way I can.

You're in my thoughts and prayers, and I hope that with time, you'll find some solace and healing.

With heartfelt sympathy,

Mrs. Darcy

The news hit me like a sledgehammer, and the pain was beyond anything I had ever felt before. It was a crushing weight on my chest, an ache that seemed to have no end. My mind was a whirlwind of emotions, each one more intense than the last. Emotions spiraled out of control, each more overwhelming than the last. It felt like my heart wasn't just broken metaphorically, but literally shattered.

"My daughter, my Ava," I sobbed, my voice breaking as I cried out in anguish. "Oh Ava, how I wish I could have died in your place."

Then, a sensation - a gentle touch on my shoulder. I turned, and there she was. Elizabeth, her eyes filled with a deep sadness that mirrored my own. "When a child is lost, the world turns cold," she whispered, her voice filled with a melancholy that sent shivers down my body.

I could feel the chill of the room intensify. Was it just my imagination, or was there an actual drop in temperature? Before I could ponder further, another presence made itself felt. Ben. His familiar hands gently cradled my face, and he pulled me close. We became a comforting tangle of shared sorrow.

His scent, earth and something more ancient, wrapped around me. "The pain of losing a child, it's a scar that never fades," he murmured into my hair, his breath cool against my ear.

A tear rolled down my cheek. It felt hot against my skin, and as it fell, it seemed to echo the depths of my despair. "Tell me about your child," I asked, needing to understand their pain.

Elizabeth's voice quivered. "I bore two children within me. One, a symbol of my love with Ben, and the other, a cruel reminder of Fredrick's malice. It felt like fate played a twisted game. My baby with Ben didn't see the world. But Peter, my child with Fredrick, he was a beacon of light in my darkest days. But that man, he hated everything that had a hint of me, including our son."

The taste of salt from my tears reached my lips, and the overwhelming bitterness mirrored the story she recounted. "One night," Elizabeth continued, her voice almost a whisper, "In his rage, Fredrick took Peter from me in the most gruesome way. He threw him into the flames."

My body tensed at the horrifying revelation. The image of such a heinous act made my stomach churn, a sour taste of bile threatening to rise.

Elizabeth, sensing my distress, tightened her grip around me. I could feel the sorrow emanating from her. "Even now," she said, her voice barely audible, "we're bound here, chained to this place by the very man who took everything from us."

Ben's touch felt colder, yet there was a gentle firmness in it that was grounding. "Every black moon night, the atrocities of the past replay, and we're left to suffer again and again."

I looked deep into his eyes, searching for answers. There was an intensity, a fire that belied the calm exterior. "What can I do? How can we end this cycle of pain?"

"There's no way Evelynn. That's the point. There's no escaping his evilness." Elizabeth's words pierced the air, filling the room with a heavy sense of hopelessness.

"We've tried everything," Ben added, his voice low and defeated. "Over the years, we've searched for answers, looked for ways to break the curse, but nothing has worked. We're trapped here."

I could feel the weight of their words crushing my spirit. The candlelight flickered, casting strange shadows on the walls. A cold draft swept through the room, making me shiver.

"But why? Why can't we fight this? Why can't

we find a way out?" My voice trembled with desperation. The taste of salt from my tears was sharp on my lips as I tried to process what they were saying.

Elizabeth looked at me, her eyes filled with sadness. "Because, Evelynn, evil like Fredrick's doesn't just go away. It lingers, it festers, and it consumes everything in its path. We've been its victims for far too long."

Ben came closer, his cold hand on my cheek. "Evelynn, we don't want you to hurt like we did. You're alone out here; come be with us."

"Ben..." My voice trailed off, not quite sure what to say. The thought of joining them, of finding peace and solace in the afterlife was tempting, especially given the feeling of emptiness that had settled over me. Yet, the very idea was also terrifying.

Their words, tinged with longing, pulled at my heart. But while a part of me yearned to be with them, another voice whispered doubts.

"I want to, but maybe I'm just too scared," I admitted.

"You're not scared, Evelynn," Ben reassured.

"You're just tired. The day's been tough on you. Just rest for now."

The room had a hushed silence, save for the distant rustling of leaves outside and our shared breaths. Their combined presence, with the touch, the scents, and the sounds, felt reassuring.They both gently helped me lie down and lay down on either side of me.

When I woke up, the room felt cold and empty. The comforting presence of Elizabeth and Ben had faded. Perhaps being with them was my fate.

But I had promised Ava I wouldn't harm myself, and I didnt want to break that promise. But without her, it felt like a huge part of me was missing.

Right then a bold idea surfaced: what if facing the monster in the manor could give me the death I was desperate for? A way to escape this miserable life once and for all.

Chapter 16

I made my way to the manor, feeling the burden of each step grow heavier. The air chilled as I approached, sending an uneasy shiver through me.

The wooden door groaned as I pushed it open, its sound reverberating in the empty halls. Inside, the air was thick and stale, permeated by the musty smell of decay and a faint, disconcerting odor of something rotten.

Though I had ventured into the manor before, tonight it took on an even more haunting guise. The flickering lantern in my hand cast creepy shadows that danced eerily across the walls, each one twisting and turning in a way that caused goosebumps to prickle on my skin.

Tonight, the manor didn't merely appear haunted; it looked as though it were drenched in sorrow. Each and every creak, whisper in the old house felt like echoes of a melancholic past.

Gathering my courage, I made my way down the corridor, the portraits of the manor's former inhabitants seemed to watch me with cold, judgmental eyes. Their faces, captured in happier times, now seemed to hold a secret sorrow, a silent testament to the tragedies that had unfolded within these walls.

Turning a corner, I entered the servants' quarters. The room was small and cramped, with simple, worn furnishings. But what caught my attention was the scene that lay before me. A woman, dressed in the tattered remnants of a maid's uniform, was cowering in the corner, her body shaking with fear. Opposite her stood a man, his posture menacing, a blood-stained knife clutched in his hand.

"You belong to me, Chloe," he hissed, his voice a mixture of anger and madness. "You think you can leave me? I'll teach you what happens to those who try."

The maid's eyes were wide with terror, but there was a defiance in her voice as she responded, "I am not yours, Ichabod. I never was. You can't control me anymore."

Enraged, Ichabod lunged at her with the knife, but Chloe, with surprising agility, dodged his attack. In a fit of rage, he struck her across the face, the force of the blow echoing through the room. She fell to the ground, her body crumpling like a broken doll.

Laughing maniacally, Ichabod continued his assault, each blow a proof of his insanity. And then, with a final act of madness, he turned the knife on himself. His body slumped to the ground, blood pooling around him.

I left the room quickly, my heart pounding in my chest, the images of violence and death imprinted in my mind.

As I continued my exploration, the manor seemed to come alive with the echoes of its dark past. In the main hallway, my footsteps reverberated through the silence, each echo a haunting reminder of the loneliness that permeated this place.

Suddenly, I felt a presence behind me. Whirling around, I came face to face with a priest, his feet dangling from a chandelier. His eyes were hollow, filled with a deep, unending sorrow.

"This place... it's cursed," he whispered, his voice barely audible. "I came to cleanse it, but the darkness... It's too strong. It consumes everything."

Before I had a chance to react, the chandelier's rope suddenly snapped, sending the priest crashing to the ground with a thud. In a moment of uncertainty, I instinctively stepped back, eager to distance myself. However, he swiftly rose to his feet and fixed his lifeless, haunting gaze directly on me. My breath caught in my throat, an instinctual scream stifled as he lunged forward, his hand swiftly covering my mouth. A wave of panic washed over me, but adrenaline kicked in. With a desperate burst of energy, I wrenched free from his grasp, my heart pounding like a drum as I dashed frantically down the hallway.

Each room I entered revealed a new horror. In one, a man lay beaten and bloodied on the floor, the victim of a violent confrontation. His assailant was a man I recognized from the paintings in the manor, a lord who had once lived here. "You thought you could steal from me and get away with it? You thief!" the lord roared, his voice seething with fury.

The man, struggling for breath, managed to choke out a plea while a piece of bread fell from his hand. "Please... I was just hungry... I needed to feed my family."

But there was no mercy to be found. The sound of bones breaking and the thief's screams echoed through the room, followed by the deafening sound of two gunshots.

Continuing my journey, I found myself in the upstairs nursery. There, a mother sat cradling the lifeless body of her child, her tears falling silently onto its pale, still face. She sang a soft, mournful lullaby, her voice filled with an unspeakable grief.

"I'm so sorry, my love," she murmured, her voice trembling with heart-wrenching sadness. "I tried so hard to save you, but I couldn't. You battled the illness for so long. Why was it not me that the sickness claimed? Why did it have to take you away?"

The pain and sorrow emanating from her was palpable, and I couldn't help but feel my own heart break at the sight.

As I went further, I saw the mother take her own life shortly after burying her child. The guilt and despair had become too much for her to bear, and she couldn't find a reason to keep living in this cursed place.

The tragedies continued to unfold before my eyes, each one more haunting than the last. And as I stood there, surrounded by the ghosts of the past, I couldn't help but feel their pain and suffering, as if it was seeping into my very being.

This manor held memories of countless agonies, all stemming from the wickedness of one man. My disdain for Fredrick grew with each thought of the torment he had caused, the anger building inside me. I headed towards the master bedroom of the manor, ready to confront the man responsible for all this suffering.

Chapter 17

THE ROOM, though silent, felt like it pulsed with a cold and foreboding energy. My instinct screamed at me to leave, but determination rooted me in place. The room's familiar scent of decay seemed to thicken, and I took a steadying breath, trying to overcome the knot of fear in my stomach.

"Coward! Show yourself!" I yelled, clenching my fists at my sides. The heavy drapes moved slightly, suggesting a presence, but no one emerged. The anticipation heightened my senses; I could hear my own heartbeat, the rustling of my flowy nightgown against my legs, and the distant cawing of a crow outside.

"Murderer!" I spat out, my voice echoing in the

room. My words seemed to provoke something in the shadows. The atmosphere grew heavier, and an oppressive feeling settled around me, making the hair on my neck stand on end.

Challenging the lurking presence further, I shouted, "Evil beast! Face me!"

The room's temperature seemed to drop even further. I could see my breath, and the chill made my skin prickle. And then, from the deepest shadows, he emerged. Frenchie's monstrous form glowed in the room's decaying grandeur. The golden carvings on his dark skin seemed to come alive, shifting and glowing, mirroring his volatile emotions. Those haunting red eyes locked onto mine, burning with anger and another emotion I couldn't quite place.

"You have the audacity to challenge me in my manor?" He roared, his voice echoing through the room, the very walls seeming to shake with its intensity. "You walk into my lair, even after I've warned you, even after I showed mercy. I can't decide if you're brave or just plain stupid."

His words ignited fury within me. In a rush of anger, I grabbed a vase from the nearby table and flung it at him. His scarlett eyes flashed with surprise. "Evelynn, test me no further, or you might regret it. Don't make me punish you."

"You mean like how you 'punished' Ben and Elizabeth?" I spat out, my voice dripping with sarcasm. "It eats you up, doesn't it? The idea that someone else could bring joy to Elizabeth when you couldn't." I was pushing him, goading him. I wanted to see the monster in him unravel.

"Don't you dare talk about things you know nothing about," he growled, stalking towards me.

I squared my shoulders and looked him in the eyes, refusing to be cowed. "Oh, but I do know you, Fredrick, Frenchie, or whatever you hide behind," I shot back, my voice echoing in the silence of the room. "I know men like you. I've come across them before. Wicked, bitter, consumed by jealousy. You deserve every bit of agony that comes your way!"

A rush of wind blew past as he lunged towards me, his speed startling. The world tilted, and suddenly I was on my back, the cold floor pressing against me. His weight bore down on me, his body trapping me. The monster's face hovered inches from mine. I could feel the heat of his breath, mingling with the cold air, creating a fog around us but I refused to turn away, meeting his fiery red gaze with my own steely determination.

But when his forked tongue unexpectedly darted out, leaving a trail of cold, slimy saliva on the scar on my cheek, I instinctively turned my head away, revulsion coursing through me. The rough fabric of my nightgown scratched against my skin as I tried to wriggle away, desperate to escape his grasp.

"You look so good under me, Evelynn. So soft, so beautiful, so pretty," he murmured, his long monstrous tongue making its way to my neck and then towards my breasts. A tingling sensation coursed through my body as I squirmed beneath him. His eyes, burning with both rage and desire, bore into mine. But when tears spilled from my eyes, his fierce expression softened, though his firm hold on me remained unyielding.

"You allowed them to touch you," he growled in my ear, his voice a dangerous mix of accusation and longing. "You sought their arms, their warmth when I could've been there for you." His hot breath brushed against my skin as he continued, "I saw them embrace you, kiss you."

His tone was possessive, jealous."Why do you care?"

His crimson eyes bore into mine, as if searching for something. Then, in a moment of vulnerability, he hesitated, and for a fleeting second, I glimpsed Frenchie's blue eyes. His guard was down, and I knew it was my chance to make a move.

Summoning all my strength, I kneeled him in the groin, causing him to release me. I knew that running was my only chance, as he was far stronger than me. With my heart pounding and a surge of adrenaline, I sprang to my feet and dashed away, the sound of my own frantic footsteps echoing through the corridor.

His footsteps pounded behind me like a menacing drumbeat, reverberating through the shadowy hallway. As I sprinted, my fingers grazed the chilly, ancient wallpaper, its texture making me shiver.

"Leave now, and I won't harm you," he called out.

"Not a chance. You'd have to kill me to get me out of here," I shot back. But then he cornered me.

I paused, ready to make a dash if I saw an opening.

"Oh, I won't kill you. But I'll make you wish I had." he snarled.

I caught sight of his massive member, and his smirk told me all I needed to know. No more waiting—I bolted. Just as I thought I'd make it to the safety of the hallway's end, his hand clamped down on my arm, stopping me cold. He whipped me around and slammed me into the wall.

Darkness swallowed my vision, blotting out the world. His voice, dripping with a predatory mix of possessiveness and menace, was the only thing that broke through. "You are mine now, my dark rose, my Evelynn. And there's no escaping me."

Chapter 18

I awoke with a throbbing headache, the pain pulsating at the back of my head. Blinking my eyes open, I stared at the unfamiliar ceiling above me, adorned with an elegant chandelier that was definitely not from my cottage. As the fog of sleep lifted, memories of the previous night flooded back, sending my heart into a frantic race.

Flashes of Frenchie, his imposing figure casting shadows in my mind, intermingled with the harrowing scenes I had witnessed at the manor. The mixture of fear and confusion from those moments surged back, igniting a sense of panic deep within me.

Hastily, I attempted to rise and sit up, but a sharp

pain in my head forced me to pause. Just then, the door swung open, revealing Frenchie. He stood in the doorway, tall and imposing, his hair tousled. He was clad in a loose white shirt, slightly unbuttoned at the top, which hung loosely on his frame, contrasting with his dark trousers.

In his hands was a tray, laden with what appeared to be breakfast. But before he could say anything, the burning anger from within pushed me forward. I got up and knocked the tray from his hands, the clattering sound as it fell to the floor echoing in the room.

With a swiftness that caught me off guard, Frenchie's fingers wrapped around strands of my hair, pulling me close. Pain shot through my scalp, my eyes watering. "Push me again, and you'll regret it," he growled, his voice dripping with warning. His breath, though he was a ghost, felt strangely warm, brushing against my face in soft gusts.

Despite the pain, I managed to retort, blinking back the tears that threatened to spill, "Like how you made Elizabeth and Ben regret their choices? What will you do to me? Torture me? Kill me? I'm not afraid of you."

His eyes locked onto mine, seething with fury and something more complicated, more raw. A smirk curved his lips, dark but oddly magnetic. "Evelynn," he said, each syllable dripping with danger. "Far worse. For all I care, my cheating wife and her lover can burn in hell. But the things I want to do with you, I can assure you, they've never crossed my thoughts for anyone else. Not in life, and certainly not in this twisted afterlife."

And then without warning, he closed the gap, slamming his lips onto mine. The unexpected ferocity of the kiss took me by surprise, and my instincts kicked in. I bit down on his lip, hard.

A muffled sound of pain and surprise left him, but it quickly turned into a chuckle. We broke apart, panting, our gazes locked.

With every ounce of defiance I could muster, I whispered, my voice shaky from the emotions coursing through me, "Do not come near me again! You wretched, fiend, ghost.. whatever monstrous entity you are."

His eyes, which had been hot with desire moments ago, now held a flash of pain. "I might be dead, and your bites and shoves might not harm me," he began, voice dripping with emotion, "But your words, Evelynn? They cut deeper than any weapon."

My chin jutted out defiantly. "Good."

The flicker of vulnerability in his eyes disappeared as quickly as it had appeared. With a quick yank on my arm, he pulled me toward him and then lowered us both to the floor, positioning me to sit between his legs. I struggled against his grip, but he held me tightly against his chest, making it clear I wasn't going anywhere.

"Since you're so hell bent on staying at my manor, you'll be following my rules. Pick up the apple slices and eat it!" he commanded, his voice firm.

My jaw set in defiance. "No! I won't."

His grip tightened, fingers digging into my arm. "You're not going anywhere. Eat it!" He grabbed a piece and moved it to my lips.

I tried to pull away, but his other hand cupped the back of my head, holding it still. Reluctantly, I opened my mouth and bit down on the apple slice. As I chewed, his hold on me relaxed slightly, yet he didn't loosen his grip.

The last piece was down, and his grip slackened. I shot up, putting space between us. He stood too, and as his boots met the floor, the sound reverberated through the empty room. His icy eyes flickered, hinting at something—amusement, maybe?

"You think acting concerned makes me forget what you are?"

"A monster? I know," he sneered. The bitterness in his words felt like sandpaper against my ears, grating and harsh.

"You're worse. You're a murderer, a child murderer!" My accusation left my lips, tasting like venom.

"Hold your tongue!" The air between us thickened, becoming electric with tension.

"The truth stings, doesn't it?" I could almost taste his rage, like burnt metal.

In a heartbeat, he was above me, pinning me to the bed. My nightgown ripped. Vulnerability washed over me.

"Stop it, Frenchie, please!" My voice broke, lost amidst the tactile sensation of fear and the guttural timbre of his breaths.

He recoiled, as if stung. His palms masked a muffled cry, a sound so desperate it filled the room. He fell to his knees with a thud that I heard through the floorboards.

"I've never—would never hurt a child," he choked out, his voice filled with a despair so palpable it was almost like another entity in the room. "I loved my son. I loved Peter so much. How can you even think I'd hurt him?" His eyes brimmed with tears.

Witnessing his vulnerability, my anger began to dissipate. The room went quiet, leaving only our breaths and a tangle of feelings. Then, he slowly got off me, his eyes meeting mine with a look of deep sorrow before he turned and left, a broken ghost seemingly lost in the echoes of his own past.

Once he was gone, I laid frozen in the bed. Lying there, trying to catch my breath, his words replayed in my mind.

I loved my son. I loved my Peter so much

I found myself wrestling with uncertainty – was he lying to me, or perhaps to himself? Could denying the truth really erase the pain? Of course, the guilt of harming his own flesh and blood would be immense, but the raw emotion in his words, the way he spoke them, it unexpectedly tugged at my heart. I took several deep breaths, trying to steady my nerves. This was no time to soften; I couldn't afford to let my guard down. I was here on a mission, after all. I needed to provoke him, to push him to the brink so he would act, so he would fulfill the grim fate I had come to meet.

I stood up and glanced at my nightgown, now reduced to tatters. Turning to the cupboard in front of me, I rummaged through its contents. My fingers brushed over various fabrics, finally coming to rest on a lavender silk gown. Though old, it exuded a sense of comfort and elegance that appealed to me in that moment. Slipping it on, the cool material hugged my body a bit more tightly than I was used to, but it'd do. As I adjusted the fit, that nagging question about Frenchie's past buzzed in my mind again. In a house swimming with secrets, the itch to dig for the truth was almost unbearable. I needed to know the truth, for my sanity, for my survival— whatever it might be.

Leaving the room, I navigated through the

hallways, now occupied by the manor's spectral inhabitants. They drifted about as if it were just another day for them. I had been in this manor before, but never had I witnessed these ghostly figures roaming so freely and randomly. I pondered what was different this time.

Despite the temptation to make eye contact, I kept my gaze firmly on the floor. I didn't want to reveal that I could see them — there was no need to invite further trouble. I quickly darted into the first room I managed to unlock, finding myself in the library. Leaning back against the door, I closed my eyes for a moment. When I opened them again, I surveyed the library. It was clean, a result of my efforts the first day I started working in the manor. My fingers idly browsed through the books until I found what I was looking for. There it was—the diary I'd spotted on my first visit. It was adorned with elegant gold embossing, and the name "Fredrick" on the cover seemed almost to beckon to me. Could this diary be the key to unraveling the complex and twisted threads of the past? I knew I had to find out.

Taking a seat, I opened the diary and skimmed

through the entries, I reached one that caught my attention.

Feb 14, 1821

Today marks a day that I will forever cherish in my heart. I met Elizabeth. Her eyes, sparkling like the brightest stars, captured my soul the moment I gazed into them. Her laughter, light and infectious, made every corner of the manor come alive. Oh, how I wish to make her the lady of this house. The bride of the manor. I dream of the days we could spend together, of children running around the corridors, filling them with joy and laughter. A hopeful future lies ahead, and I yearn for the day I can call her mine. If only mother and father were here to witness this. They would have adored her just as I do.

December 24, 1821

Despair clouds my mind today. The image haunts me—Elizabeth, entangled in another man's embrace. The very thought pierces my heart like a thousand knives. What have I done to deserve such betrayal? Have I not provided for her? Showered her with love and gifts? Am I not man enough for her? My heart feels heavy, weighed down by the burden of failure as a husband. But I shall not give up. I'll win back her heart, talk to her, make her understand. She must see that my love for her is true and unchanging.

January 4, 1822

Betrayal. The word lingers in my mind, taunting me, reminding me of the promises broken. Elizabeth vowed to me, looked me in the eyes, and swore she wouldn't see him again. But today, as she entered, her disheveled appearance gave away her deceit. I tried, oh how I tried, to love her, to make her forget her lover. To make her see that my love for her was pure. Yet, she lies to me. Each glance, each touch from her feels like deceit. The pain is unbearable. Yet, a glimmer of hope remains. I will try, one last time, to win back the heart of the woman I so dearly love.

Feb 14, 1822

A year. A whole year since the day we vowed to stand by each other's side. But now, the walls of this manor whisper secrets and lies. They tell tales of Elizabeth's betrayal, of her longing for another. The maids, the servants, their eyes are filled with pity when they look my way. I despise it, every lingering gaze that suggests they know something I don't. A man's pride and honor are all he has, and mine seems to be slipping through my fingers like sand. I approached Elizabeth, hoping words of love would mend what was broken. But she remained cold, distant, and every denial from her felt like a knife to my heart.

Feb 20, 1822
Every moment, every day, her lies weigh on me. Love, it seems, has a cruel way of turning to anguish. I see her lost in thoughts of someone else. And though she denies it, I know. I can feel the truth in the very air of the manor. I have tried force, tried to make her see reason, to make her understand the depth of my pain. But to no avail. Her heart is elsewhere, with someone else, and it's tearing me apart.

April 25, 1822
The masquerade ball. A night that promised

laughter and joy turned into one of pain and betrayal. I saw her, slipping away with a stranger, the shadows cloaking their deceit. When I confronted her, the evidence was clear —the smudged lip rouge, the flushed cheeks, the swollen lips. In a moment of blind rage, I struck her. The weight of my action, the realization of what I had done, crushed me. To punish myself for the unforgivable act, I seared my palm, letting the burn remind me of my own weakness. Yet, the physical pain was nothing compared to the agony of her betrayal.

June 12, 1822

After the masquerade ball, Elizabeth became somewhat distant from me. However, in May, I received the most wonderful news of all – Elizabeth is expecting a child. We had shared a night together just before the masquerade, and I sincerely hope and believe that this child is mine. I trust that Elizabeth wouldn't intentionally hurt me like this. Perhaps this child will serve as a catalyst to mend our relationship. When Elizabeth becomes a mother and I become a father, it's possible that she'll view life through a new and different lens. I can't express how eagerly I await the arrival of this baby, longing for the opportunity to embrace fatherhood with her.

As my fingers skimmed the timeworn pages of Fredrick's diary, it was like flipping through a narrative at odds with itself. Elizabeth had spoken of a loveless marriage, a trap with her as the unwilling prey. Fredrick, though, sketched a love story soured by betrayal. So who was playing a role? Was Elizabeth just acting, spinning sad tales to win sympathy? Or had Fredrick been a lovesick fool, blind to his own mistakes?

Closing the diary, my thoughts whirled. The Fredrick described on these pages was far from a monster; he was a man full of emotion and touched by heartbreak. But then again, Elizabeth's voice, dripping with pain, still echoed in my ears, speaking of a life she hadn't chosen.

I put the diary back on the shelf, feeling uneasy. It was as if the manor itself was a maze, its walls echoing with conflicting stories. And there I was, stuck in the middle, trying to sift through the confusion to find what was real.

Chapter 19

B Y THE TIME I left the library, the sun had already set, and the warm glow from the stars filled the sky. I knew I needed to go back to the room instantly. I didn't want to come across Frenchie's monstrous form.

But just as I climbed the stairs, a blood-curdling scream echoed through the manor. I raced towards the sound, ending up on a moonlit balcony. There, I saw a sight I'd never forget: Frenchie in absolute torment, his form shifting and contorting painfully.

I stood there, unsure of my next move, feeling a sense of paralysis in my limbs. I wanted to run but something inexplicable held me in place. Seeing him in so much pain tugged at my heart and my hand went to my mouth seeing the horror unfolding before me. Frenchie spotted me and let out a low growl, his message direct and unmistakable. "Evelynn, go to the master bedroom and lock the door."

Filled with fear, I nodded and took a step back. The sound of Frenchie's bones snapping and reshaping, his form growing larger, filled me with dread. I knew I had to run. Just as I began to turn away, a strong hand grabbed me by the throat and lifted me off the ground, cutting off my escape.

I recognized the vile man instantly. It was that maid, Chloe's husband. Ichabod. He appeared utterly repulsive and revolting. The skin on his face oozed with pus, and his toothless mouth emitted a stench of spoiled meat.

"So, we meet again," he remarked with a smirk on his face. "Remember that time when I chased you with a knife? Your screams were like music to me. How about an encore?" He leaned in closer, and my skin crawled.

But then his grip on my throat loosened. It was as though his hand had been cut off. In fact, it had been. His body was flung across the balcony, a lifeless heap. Frenchie stood there, transformed and terrifying, his eyes filled with fire.

"She's mine!" Frenchie roared, his voice echoing through the corridor.

Ichabod tried to crawl away, but Frenchie was on him in an instant. "How dare you lay a hand on her," Frenchie growled, his voice laced with a ferocity I had never heard before. I watched in horror as Frenchie clawed at Ichabod with his sharp claws, tearing him to shreds. The cries from Ichabod were so piercingly loud that I instinctively covered my ears with my hands and tightly shut my eyes.

When I felt a hand on my shoulder, I cautiously opened my eyes. It was Frenchie, his red eyes fixed on me.

"I thought he was going to...going to kill me," I stammered, even though I had come here seeking death. But the idea of dying at the hands of that repulsive creature sent a shiver down my spine.

My words had barely left my lips when Ichabod started pulling himself back together. The pieces of his body reattached seamlessly, and he became whole again, as if nothing had occurred. Observing his surroundings and spotting Frenchie, Ichabod swiftly made his escape from the balcony.

I couldn't believe my eyes, and I turned to Frenchie, asking in utter astonishment, "How is that even possible?"

Frenchie's head hung low, and I observed as the glyphs on his body shifted restlessly. They always seemed to respond to his emotions. He settled onto the cement bench on the balcony, gazing up at the moon. "Evelynn, this place... It is like a Limbo. Each soul is trapped. They can be hurt, but they will become whole again, and the torment starts anew." He explained, his voice heavy with a deep sadness. "You saw the priest hanging, the mother crying for her child, the man killing a thief and turning the knife on himself, Chloe being killed by her husband, and me changing into this monster. All souls here relive some form of agony."

Even in the open air, I felt a suffocating weight hearing his words. "Limbo? Souls? How did I become entangled in all of this? Why am I able to see all this?" I questioned, more to myself than him.

Frenchie's monstrous form seemed to soften, and his enormous paw-like hand gently enveloped mine. My hand looked almost childlike in comparison. "Your pain, your overwhelming emotions are like a beacon, drawing you closer to this realm of despair," he explained. "I can sense... There's something profoundly troubling you, Evelynn. Something gnawing at you from within. Why did you come here? I understand you wanted to confront me, but I sense there's more. Please, tell me," Frenchie implored, his eyes searching mine.

I took a deep breath, allowing the storm of emotions to pour out. The haunting words of the letter had been a catalyst for my despair. Facing Frenchie, my voice shook as I revealed my darkest thoughts. "I came here to end the pain. I thought by provoking you, making you angry, you might put an end to this torturous existence of mine."

His eyes, earnest and understanding, met mine, offering solace to the turmoil within. "Evelynn," he spoke softly, "I could never harm you. Never."

I wiped away my tears, but they continued to flow. Placing my hand over my heart, I pressed it tightly, for that's where the pain seemed most intense. My heart was breaking. "But it hurts. It hurts so much. My life feels meaningless, " I confessed.

Frenchie drew closer, gently taking my hand and pulling me closer to him. I allowed it, my heart heavy with the weight of my pain. "Perhaps I can offer you some solace, Evelynn," he suggested tenderly. "Help you forget, even if just for a while."

His words hung heavily in the air, thick with emotion. In a hushed tone, barely more than a whisper, I asked, "Really? Can you help me forget? Can you make this pain go away?"

His intense gaze stirred something deep within me. He leaned closer, our faces nearly touching. "I..I want to," Frenchie whispered, his voice trembling. "Anything to make you feel better. But I can't help but fear... what if I end up causing you more harm? After all, I am a monster."

Despite my fears, I found strength in my vulnerability. "I believe you won't," I whispered back. "But know this: when the sun rises, my contempt for you remains. Yet, at this moment, I need this. I need you."

A hint of his usual smirk flickered across his face. "That's a risk I'm more than willing to take," he murmured.

My eyes locked with Frenchie's—an intense, unbreakable bond that transcended the physical. His gaze burned with such intensity that it made my body tingle and my heart race. A powerful wave of desire coursed through me as I stepped closer, feeling his warmth radiating from his ebony skin and his breath coming out in short, excited pants. Frenchie's hands caressed my curves gently as he scooped me up. As we made our way from the balcony towards the bedroom, my eyes remained fixed on his scarlet ones. Despite his monstrous appearance that had frightened me before, at that moment, all I could see was how much he wanted to take care of me.

Once inside the master bedroom, Frenchie gently laid me on the bed, his intense red eyes searing through me with scorching heat. Our lips met in a passionate embrace, igniting shivers of pleasure throughout my curvy body. His sharp teeth nibbed at my lower lip and his hands roamed my form, discovering every contour and inch of my flesh. As he explored, he softly whispered, "Every part of you is like discovering a masterpiece."

He entwined our hands, and the sensation of his

cool skin against mine sent a shiver up my spine. His voice, husky with desire, murmured, "You're everything I've ever wanted, and more."

I locked my gaze deeply into his eyes, torn between a flood of emotions I couldn't quite put into words. At that moment, I realized I didn't fully understand what I was feeling for him. All I knew was that I wanted him—I needed him.

He slowly removed my clothing, his movements both experienced and passionate. As he traced his claw-like nails along the contours of my waist, goosebumps erupted all over my body. His touch was electrifying, reigniting a fire inside my belly that had remained dormant for years.

My breath hitched and as I opened my mouth, Frenchie crashed his lips over mine in an almost feral manner, passionately devouring my mouth as if it was our first kiss. His tongue explored my mouth, teasing my tongue and tasting my lips. I responded eagerly, moaning into his mouth as the fire within me continued to rage. His breath sent ripples of pleasure through me, and I was acutely aware of his body—all hard edges and muscles and strength.

He pulled away from the kiss and looked into my eyes. "Tell me you want this. I will stop if you have second thoughts."

I hesitated for a few seconds but then shook my head and said, "Don't stop. I want this. I want this so badly, Frenchie." Lifting my head, I wrapped my arms around his neck and pulled him closer. His face found its place on my chest, and he started to plant affectionate kisses over my breasts. Even in his monstrous form, he remained gentle, handling me delicately, as if I were a fragile doll.

His kisses continued to travel, moving down towards my belly, and then lower, which caught me by surprise. "What... what are you doing?" I asked, my confusion evident.

He chuckled softly. "You think I won't taste the nectar?"

"Nectar?" I asked, still puzzled. I had no idea what he meant, but when his tongue swiped there, I felt electric shocks coursing through my body.

With a deliberate slowness, he began his first long, languid lick over my core, tracing from the base of my entrance to up and over my nub. His tongue left no spot untouched, ensuring that every inch received its share of his attention.

"Oh, my... Frenchie, you don't have to do this. I'm not sure if it's right," I said, my confusion evident as I hesitated.

He paused briefly, looking at me with a hint of desire in his eyes, and then he licked again. "How does it feel?" he asked, his voice husky with anticipation.

I let out a breathless moan. "Ah... it feels like heaven," I replied, the intensity of the moment overwhelming my doubts.

He leaned in close, his lips brushing against my ear as he whispered, "If something feels so divine, so incredibly good, how can it not be right?"

Driven by an insatiable hunger, Frenchie moved back down, his face between my legs and continued to suck and lick my core with such fervor that it pushed me to the edge within mere minutes. The more I moaned and writhed, the more voracious he became. After a while, my fingers clutched tightly onto his horns, and his hips instinctively started thrusting against nothingness. He growled and snarled against my core lips, allowing his nose to nudge at my nub, intensifying the sensations.

"Oh, Frenchie... Frenchie... Don't stop," I pleaded, even though deep down, I knew he had no intention of stopping.

As he continued to lick, I felt something snap inside me. I curled my toes and let out a wanton moan, lost in the overwhelming pleasure that coursed through my body. It was as if I were on cloud nine, and the world around me faded away. I saw stars in front of my eyes as my breath quickened.

After a moment, Frenchie lifted himself up, his face glistening with desire and satisfaction, hovering over me. I pulled him close to me, our lips meeting in a passionate kiss, savoring the taste of my own desire on his tongue. As we finally pulled apart, our breaths mingling, I looked into his eyes, my heart racing.

"It was... It was perfect. I've never felt that way before. I thought my heart was stopping," I admitted, my voice filled with awe.

He chuckled softly and looked at me with intense longing. "Evelynn, I can't believe a woman as incredible as you hasn't experienced that kind of bliss before. I want to spend every second of my existence giving you pleasure," he vowed, his words filled with devotion.

Before I could react to his words, he settled himself between my legs and looked at me, his eyes searching mine, and asked, "Still sure you want this?"

This time, there was no hesitation, not even for a second. "I want it like air to breathe," I affirmed with unwavering conviction.

A smile formed on his lips and entered me filling me to the brim. "Do you like this?" he asked.

I nodded, my breaths heavy, "I love it."

Frenchie then lifted my foot to his mouth, biting my toe. I squirmed, but he held it there. At this angle, he was deep inside me.

We moved together in a passionate embrace. I felt a connection like I had never known before—I was being pulled in by his gaze. With each breath, the fire between us grew, and I felt myself melting into him. All I wanted was to be in his embrace forever, losing myself in his depths. He murmured, "You're the missing piece I've been searching for," and suddenly I felt my body unravel once more, and I found myself immersed in a state of nirvana unlike anything I had ever experienced before.

Following me, Frenchie came with a roar, so loud and so powerful that the intensity of our passion swallowed the entire space around us.

We were both spent and lay in each other's arms, breathing in the quiet after the storm. I felt deeply satisfied and soon my eyes grew heavy and I drifted off to sleep.

Chapter 20

AS THE AFTERNOON light filtered through the velvet curtains, my eyes fluttered open. Lying beside me was Frenchie, his eyes closed in peaceful slumber. Even in death, his golden-brown beard and tousled blonde curls made him incredibly handsome.

Carefully, I combed my fingers through his hair. Feeling the touch, he stirred slightly, prompting me to sit back and hug my knees to my chest.

Breaking the silence, I spoke, "I never realized ghosts could sleep."

His eyes gradually opened, revealing a softness that came from just waking, and he replied, his voice a murmur, "I haven't slept in almost a century. It's the first time I've truly slept. I can't explain it, but it's as if a spell has been cast upon me, and my long-silent heart finds solace only in your presence."

My heart swelled at his words. "Don't say such things, Frenchie. Last night-" I trailed off as I looked at the window.

Frenchie's eyes widened in concern, sitting up so quickly it made my head spin. "Did I hurt you, Evelynn?" His hands flew to my face, gently touching it, then darted down to my arms and legs, looking for any sign of injury.

His gaze finally landed on the faint scars on my chest, scars he'd given me on that fateful night in the manor. His eyes filled with regret.

"You didn't hurt me," I said, grabbing his hand that was checking the old scars. "Last night was, well, just perfect. You were wild, but in the best way. I'm still trying to make sense of everything that happened, that's all."

His eyes met mine, searching. "Evelynn, being this close to someone, feeling almost human again even if it's just for a second—it's something I've waited for, for so long. You make it possible. This might not last forever, but know this: my heart, as still as it is, beats only for you. You're so captivating, and strong; it's like you light a fire in me that makes me want to just consume you entirely."

I hesitated, my fingers unconsciously tracing the scar on my cheek. "But why me, Frenchie? Look at me. I'm not conventionally pretty."

"That scar," he said softly, his eyes reflecting a deep admiration, "it tells a story of resilience and strength. It's a mark of your courage, evidence of the fact that what didn't kill you has only made you stronger. You are a remarkable woman, Evelynn."

As he continued to speak, his fingers traced circles on my arm, a soothing sensation that seemed to awaken something within me. It was as if every touch held a promise of something more, something inexplicably tender and real.

"You love me that much?" I marveled, the warmth of his affection washing over me like a gentle tide.

"More than words can explain. Trust me, if I were alive," he declared, his voice trembling with emotions, "I'd cherish you every minute of the day. I'd make you my bride."

"Your bride," I repeated. "Frenchie, I... I don't know how to feel. It's all so confusing."

Frenchie sensed my inner turmoil and responded with understanding, "Evelynn, it's okay to feel this way. It's okay to be confused."

I held the sheets a little tighter around me, my gaze turned inward. "It's not that simple."

My words were cut short when I heard the sound of a child laughing in the big halls. I sat up fast. "Did you hear that?" I asked Frenchie.

"Hear what?" He asked, looking puzzled.

"A child's laugh. There's a child in the manor," I told him. But he still looked lost.

Not waiting any longer, I grabbed the sheet to cover myself and hopped out of bed, following the sound of laughter.

It led me to a dimly lit room, the air pregnant with anticipation. And there, unfolding before my eyes, was a scene from the past. I felt like a fly on the wall.

Elizabeth, her once-elegant dress now torn and disheveled, paced the room in a frenzy. Her cascading golden hair framed a face twisted with desperation. The window creaked open, and in slipped Ben, his rugged features aglow with longing and desire.

"Elizabeth," he breathed, drawing her close, their lips meeting in a desperate kiss.

Elizabeth pulled away abruptly, her voice laced with worry. "This is dangerous, Ben."

Before Ben could respond, a bubbly giggle broke the tension. A little boy, no more than three years old, rushed in, heading straight for Elizabeth. But instead of embracing him, she harshly pushed him away.

"Stay away from me you demon spawn!" she hissed at her own child.

The child stumbled, landing at the feet of another figure who had just entered the room—Frenchie.

In a frenzy of emotion, Frenchie's face twisted with rage as he launched himself at Ben. The room became a battleground as they fought with unrestrained ferocity. Fists met flesh as Frenchie's punches landed, and Ben retaliated with swift kicks. The clash of their bodies led them perilously close to the balcony's edge, and in a fateful moment, Ben lost his balance and tumbled over the railing.

A shocked gasp escaped Frenchie's lips as he watched Ben's fall. He stood there in a daze, his eyes wide with disbelief, before collapsing to his knees. His trembling hands clawed at his face as he grappled with the weight of what had just occurred.

"Oh dear lord! What have I done? I killed a man." Frenchie's voice cracked with hysteria, his words a desperate chant of disbelief and guilt.

Amidst the chaos, Elizabeth burst into the balcony, her arrival marked by a piercing shriek that echoed like a banshee's wail. Her eyes bore into Frenchie with seething hatred as she spat out her words like venom. "You'll pay for this!"

Before my eyes, the scene shifted, and I found myself witnessing a heart-wrenching tragedy. The young and innocent Peter was engrossed in his toys, oblivious to the impending horror. With a sudden and chilling quickness, Elizabeth grabbed her own son, her eyes vacant, and her face streaked with tears.

"Mummy, where are you taking me?" Peter's innocent voice quivered with confusion, his trusting eyes searching for answers. But Elizabeth remained ominously silent.

She led him into a foreboding, dark basement and firmly locked the door behind them. The atmosphere in the room grew suffocatingly heavy as I watched, unable to intervene.

Elizabeth's once-loving face contorted with anger and sinister determination as she opened a grimoire, its ancient pages crackling with dark energy. I recognized it instantly—a Grimoire. The gravity of the situation weighed down on me, and I felt helpless as I watched this horrifying scene unfold.

As Elizabeth started her chilling chant, "O custos inferni. immolo carnem meam et sanguinem, qui te advocet," her voice resonated with power, invoking dark forces. The wind outside began to howl and rage, as if in response to her invocation. The very ground beneath me quaked, and it felt as though the world itself was trembling in fear.

I could hear Frenchie bang the door. "Please Elizabeth, leave Peter out of it." He begged from the other side, but Elizabeth stayed steadfast in her incantation, her voice growing stronger with each passing moment. "Da mihi et dilecto meo vitam aeternam et tuam famem explebo. Adiuva me in ultione mea, et te praestabo tristibus animis."

The room filled with a palpable dread, the air thickening. I was paralyzed with horror as she took Peter in her arms and hurled him into the furnace. His screams echoed until they were finally extinguished, leaving silence.

Just then, Frenchie burst into the basement. His eyes widened at the scene before him. Filled with rage, he lunged at Elizabeth, grabbing her by the throat. "You've taken my son from me. I'll kill you," he seethed. A laugh escaped Elizabeth and Frenchie's eyes widened with rage. He squeezed her throat hard and Elizabeth's eyes rolled to the back of her head. He then let her go and she abruptly collapsed, lifeless.

Overcome with anguish, Frenchie fell to his knees, his cries filling the room like those of a wounded animal. Tears flowed down my cheeks as well; the weight of the past was too much to bear.

Suddenly, the scenery changed. I found myself in a forest, a flickering fire in the distance casting unsettling shadows. I realized I was seeing through my own eyes when I noticed my bloodied hands. Lying before me was Frenchie's lifeless body.

"No!" I screamed, my voice tinged with despair.

Almost as if possessed, my hands began to move of their own accord. I carved unfamiliar symbols into Frenchie's flesh while muttering incantations I didn't understand. Dragging his lifeless body to the edge of a gaping pit, I looked down for a moment before tossing him in. "Now he can be with his son," I heard myself say coldly.

And as I stood there, on the edge of that pit, the devastation of what had happened started to sink in and it was almost too much for me to bear.

Moments later the vision gradually faded and I felt utterly shaken and breathless. Looking around I found myself in Frenchie's arm, his eyes on me with concern. "What did you see?"

My voice quivered as I responded, "Too much, Frenchie. Too much."

Chapter 21

I TOLD FRENCHIE everything I had seen. He sat in a chair, looking out the window, lost in his own thoughts. "Frenchie, you've been silent about your pain for so long. In my visions, you suffer, and in one of them I am the one causing it!"

He finally turned to me, his eyes meeting mine. With a sad smile and a shake of his head, he said, "Evelynn, I can't imagine you ever hurting me."

I moved closer to him, kneeling down and taking his hand gently into my own. I kissed it, my lips barely grazing his skin. "Frenchie, what about the visions? They're haunting me. That stormy night, I saw you, Elizabeth, and Ben. I saw the scene with the childbirth and how Elizabeth lost one of her babies. And now, what happened today... What does it all mean?"

But he didn't say anything.

Annoyed by his silence once again, I stood up and started pacing the room. Back and forth, back and forth, as if the motion could magically conjure up the answers I was desperate for. Why wasn't he saying anything? His quietness felt like a wall between us, and I was left grappling with my thoughts, alone.

"Speak to me, Frenchie. I feel like I'm stuck in a maze of confusion. I need you to help me see the way out," I pleaded, my voice carrying an edge of desperation.

Frenchie finally broke his silence, his voice like a steady anchor in a stormy sea. "You told me your visions, they're connected to your emotional state, Evelynn. Ever since you lost your daughter, the spirit realm has been more active around you, hasn't it?"

I stopped in my tracks, my eyes meeting his. "Yes, that's exactly it."

Frenchie's eyes seemed to wander, but not aimlessly. It was as if he were sifting through the very sands of time. "Let me ask you, what does 'the past' mean to you?"

I thought for a moment, my heart still racing but my mind more focused. "It's our history, Frenchie. Our life story written in invisible ink."

His eyes locked onto mine, piercing yet gentle. "Consider this—history, in a way, is like a ghost, always hovering, influencing our choices, our lives." The clarity his words provided felt like a lighthouse cutting through a foggy night. Our pasts were not just chapters in a book; they were specters, shaping our present and casting shadows on our future.

"Frenchie, it's time. I need to know your story, and not through rumors or idle talk. Let's open up this book of secrets. Please, for both our sakes."

His eyes were a tumult of emotions, each one flowing into the next, until he gave a nod, as if agreeing not just to share his story, but to let go of something heavy he'd been carrying. In that nod, it was clear—unraveling the threads of his past was the next crucial step for both of us, a way to make sense of the haunting visions and the enigmatic world that seemed to be drawing us ever closer.

Chapter 22

SITTING IN THE library, the air hung heavy with the weight of countless secrets, and I found myself drawn into Frenchie's eyes, which were glowing orbs of untold despair. He sat opposite me, his gaze fixed on the crackling fire, and I could see the lines of sorrow etched into every contour of his face. He looked at his diary and I knew that revisiting the painful chapters of his life would inevitably stir up old wounds, but my need for understanding compelled me to push forward.

I had been quick to judge, to believe the accusations against Frenchie, to vilify him in my mind. Yet, here I was, seeking his story, yearning to uncover the truths that had remained buried for far too long.

"I was once the happiest man, Evelynn," he began, his voice trembling with memories that had haunted him for centuries. "Before Elizabeth came into my life, this mansion was a sanctuary of joy and laughter. My mother's dying wish was for me to fill this grand house with love, and for a while, I genuinely believed I was doing just that."

I could sense the warmth in his voice, the longing for a time when Blackwood Manor had been a place of hope and happiness.

"Elizabeth," he continued, a bittersweet smile tugging at the corners of his lips, "she was a force of nature, utterly irresistible. We were deeply in love—or so I believed. But then something changed. She grew cold, distant."

His eyes, once radiant with the memory of their love, now dimmed with the pain of betrayal.

My heart ached for him. To love so profoundly, only to witness it crumble—it was a nightmare I wouldn't wish upon anyone.

"Then came the twins," he said, his voice quivering with emotion as he spoke of their children. "One of them was not mine. When that child passed away, Elizabeth blamed me for everything, even things beyond my control. It was later revealed that she had been ensnared by dark magic through her lover, Ben."

The room seemed to constrict around us, the weight of his words pressing down like a heavy shroud.

I could almost see the specter of the man he once was, a man who had loved and lost, and then lost even more.

"One fateful night, everything reached a breaking point. Ben fell from the balcony during a heated argument. Elizabeth laid the blame squarely on my shoulders, and—," he paused, his voice trembling, "—she killed our other child, Peter."

His admission was filled with the agonizing weight of guilt, guilt that had haunted him for centuries.

At this point, tears welled up in my eyes, and I reached out to grasp his hand, offering what little comfort I could.

"I strangled her, Evelynn," he confessed, his voice barely more than a whisper, filled with profound remorse. "In a blind frenzy of rage and grief, I ended her life. But by the time I realized what I had done, she was already gone. In the days that followed, I was consumed by despair, and I took my own life."

The room seemed to grow even colder, the gravity of his confession hanging heavy in the air.

He paused again, taking a deep, shuddering breath. "I believed it was the end. By taking my own life, I thought I had finally escaped my torment. But I awoke as if from a deep slumber, only to find myself back in this mansion. I cried out, but no one heard me. I watched in horror as Ichabod killed Chloe, and she, too, joined this side. And then, the black moon appeared."

Frenchie's eyes lost focus, as if he were transported back to those nightmarish moments. "Evelynn, you must understand, Halloween nights are peculiar enough, but a Black Moon Halloween? It's an entirely different beast. It's as if the rare celestial alignment amplifies the power of malevolent entities. Yet, there's one entity, in particular, that claims this mansion as its hunting ground."

He turned to me, his eyes filled with the torment

of countless years. "This entity isn't just a haunting; it's predatory. It's drawn to the cries of despair, the tears of sorrow. It thrives on them, needing them to sustain its dark existence."

His words weighed heavily in the air, each syllable sinking like a stone in a still pond, muddying the atmosphere even further.

"It emerges when there's a Black Moon on Halloween night, as if the rare alignment enhances its dreadful influence," Frenchie continued. "Imagine being a soul imprisoned here. Every cry you release, every scream you muster, it all nourishes this entity. You're not merely haunted; you're hunted."

He leaned in closer, his voice dropping to a mere whisper, as if afraid the very walls might bear witness to his words. "What makes it even more harrowing is that on Halloween night, the souls are stronger, more tangible. They experience greater pain, deeper despair, and that only makes them a richer feast for this entity."

Frenchie sighed deeply, his eyes finally meeting mine, and I could see the torment etched into every line of his face. "It's as if it's a gourmet meal for this malevolent being. A banquet of misery, arranged to its liking. It doesn't merely force them to relive their darkest moments; it revels in their torment. It feasts on their suffering."

Once he was done, my mind was reeling, struggling to comprehend the darkness that had consumed this place for generations. I couldn't help but empathize with Frenchie, trapped in an unending cycle of anguish and torment, all because of a love that had spiraled into betrayal and despair.

Chapter 23

HEARING FRENCHIE'S TALE cracked something open inside me. Here was a man, haunted in more ways than one, wearing the scars of a love gone awry. "Frenchie, if there's any hope, I'm going to find it. I saw Elizabeth's curse—you don't deserve this for eternity. I need to get to your grave. I can break the spell; I can free you."

His eyes softened, yet hesitation shadowed them. "You're putting yourself on the line. As long as you're alive, the entity can't harm you, and I want to keep it that way."

"But... but I want to help you, Frenchie," I said.

He shook his head and grabbed my shoulders. "Evelynn, don't try to be a saint."

That was the tipping point for me. Anger surged through my veins, and I couldn't contain it any longer. "Don't you dare label my caring as some saintly act!"

Stung by my own outburst, I retreated to the master bedroom. My thoughts swirled as thick as the tears running down my face. There was a soft knock.

"I'm sorry," Frenchie's voice trickled through the door, filled with concern. "I don't understand why the 'saint' comment hurts you so much."

I wiped my eyes hastily. "Because, wanting to help you isn't saintly; it's human. Why is it so hard for you to trust that I want to help you? That I care."

His eyes found mine, warm but hesitant. "Evelynn, it's not that I don't trust you. It's just... I've already lost more than a man should bear. The thought of losing you too terrifies me. I'd face that entity every day for eternity to keep you safe."

My defenses crumbled. "Why? Why go to such lengths?"

He stepped closer, his eyes never leaving mine. "Because, Evelynn, I love you."

The world stood still. And as if pulled by an unseen force, I leaned in and our lips met. Breathing heavily, I whispered, "Please, make love to me."

Frenchie, his eyes searching mine, asked softly, "To help you forget the pain?"

"No, because I crave it all, Frenchie—the heat of your touch, your love, every last bit of you!" As the words burst from my lips, Frenchie closed the distance between us. His lips trailed down my neck, sending shudders through my body. My heart raced as I felt his hands caress my body, his touch sending sparks of desire through me.

As he kissed my lips, I could feel the intense heat between us. My body responded eagerly, arching towards him as his hands expertly touched my curves. As his fingers began to work the laces of my gown, I stiffened.

He paused, eyes searching my face. "What's wrong?"

"I can't," I stammered, glancing at the bright afternoon light filtering in through the window. "The gown stays. I... I can't. Last night it was dark... But right now, in the light, I just can't. I'm self-conscious about my body."

With a warm smile, he leaned in close, his beard lightly brushing against my skin. "Let me show you that you're perfect, just the way you are," he whispered, his voice tinged with love. He kissed his way down my body, leaving a trail of soft kisses on my skin. I closed my eyes, surrendering to his touch, as he slowly removed my dress, revealing my nakedness to him.

He sat me on the edge of the bed and gently turned me to face the full-length mirror. "Look at yourself, my love,". I opened my eyes and gazed at my reflection in the mirror. I expected to see all my imperfections, but all I saw was beauty.

With gentle hands, he undid the rest of my clothes, slowly stripping me of every barrier between us. I felt exposed, vulnerable, yet incredibly alive and desirable. Frenchie's fingers explored every inch of my body, tracing every curve, every dip and hollow. I couldn't help but moan under his touch, my body responding with every kiss, every caress.

"You're more captivating than Aphrodite, and yet you carry a strength that rivals Athena's. In my eyes, you eclipse them all," Frenchie whispered, his voice thick with emotion. And then he took me, his love and passion filling every inch of my being. As I looked at my reflection in the mirror, I truly felt like what Frenchie saw me as—a goddess.

Chapter 24

WITH FRENCHIE ASLEEP beside me, I eased out of bed and quickly dressed. The sun was on the brink of setting, and time was ticking. Ever since I'd seen myself carving those markings into Frenchie's skin, a gut feeling told me the curse was linked to his dead body in some way. Grabbing a shovel from the manor's storeroom, I made my way from the manor to the graveyard. The wind whispered secrets, and the leaves rustled as if they were in on some big cosmic joke. As I reached the rows of timeworn tombstones, my heart pounded in anticipation.

Cold air turned my breath to mist as I scoured the graveyard, finally finding the tombstone marked

"Fredrick Blackwood."

"I swear I'll break this curse, Frenchie," I muttered under my breath.

Time blurred as I dug into the earth, my shovel hitting the ground over and over. Sweat dripped, and my muscles ached, but I kept going. At last, the shovel clanged against wood. I'd found it—a worn-out coffin, its wood aged by time.

As I lifted the lid with trembling hands, dread filled me. The coffin was empty!

Where could his body be?

My head spun with fear and confusion when a sudden, brutal impact struck me on the back of the head and I blacked out.

I woke up, disoriented, in the sprawling garden of the manor. Thorny roses and overgrown ivy surrounded me, making the place look both wild and trapped, like my feelings at that moment. I glanced up to see the black moon, hidden behind wisps of cloud, casting a glow over the area. I was bound by ropes, arms tied behind my back, unable to move.

Elizabeth and Ben emerged from behind a large,

twisted oak. They wore triumphant smiles, like predators closing in on prey. Behind them, Frenchie, transformed into his monstrous form, looked like a tormented soul. A guttural, agonized howl escaped his lips. It was evident he was in pain, restrained not by physical chains but by the magic Elizabeth was channeling to keep him immobilized.

"Let her go Elizabeth. You hate me. Keep Evelynn out of it!" Frenchie roared in between his howls, his voice laced with a despair I'd never heard before.

Elizabeth's eyes locked with mine and without even looking in Frenchie's direction, she waved her hand, and Frenchie was hurled into a nearby tree. He crashed against the bark, struggling and writhing but unable to free himself.

"No! Don't hurt him!" I screamed.

"You should worry about yourself, love. Tell me, why didn't you end your miserable, sad life when you had the chance?" she asked, seeming bored.

Feeling my heart pound, I managed to ask, "Why do you even care about my life? What's in it for you?"

"Your deep-rooted sorrow and despair made you an ideal sacrifice for the demon we serve," she sneered, savoring my shock. "A soul saturated in misery is a delicacy to him."

Ben moved closer to Elizabeth and planted a kiss on her lips. "Now, it's almost time. With the black moon in the sky, the demon will come himself to claim her soul."

Realization hit me. Fredrick and Peter were not the only victims of Elizabeth. She had been the one driving people to suicide? Coaxing them into killing themselves and others, all to harvest souls for a demon!

"So it was you, pulling the strings behind people's misery, just to feed that demon!" I exclaimed, shocked to the core.

"Exactly," Elizabeth fired back, her eyes twinkling wickedly as if my horror was the missing spice in her twisted recipe. "People are filled with despair, you know? They just need a little push to tip them over. Like the one we gave you." She laughed, a sound so unsettling it made my skin crawl.

My brows furrowed, confusion clouding my

thoughts.

Elizabeth smirked, flicking her wrist as if dismissing something trivial. "You're more naive than we thought, Evelynn. When you first set foot here, we knew you were the perfect sacrifice. We figured you might even do the deed yourself. But when you saw Frenchie's monstrous form and tried to leave, we had to step in."

She paused, pacing around me as she continued, "That's when we trapped you here with a powerful spell. Oh, and we entangled you in our twisted love story, hoping you'd reach the edge and jump off yourself. But you didn't."

Stopping to lean in close, her eyes narrowed, she added, "You remember that letter, don't you? You spilled your life story to us, giving us everything we needed to craft that fake letter, hoping it would push you to end your own life. But alas, you proved more stubborn than we thought."

The weight of her words crushed me. Ava, my daughter, was alive. They'd lied, made up a story so cruel.

"Why?" I managed to choke out, as tears blurred my vision.

"Fredrick took my love from me that fateful night. But by sacrificing Peter, I brought him back," she revealed, a grim satisfaction creeping into her tone. "I struck a deal with a force beyond your comprehension. It didn't just grant us eternal life, but endless wealth, too."

Pausing, she moved even closer, her eyes locking onto mine, searching for a reaction. "By the time Fredrick strangled me, the pact was already sealed. To the world, Ben and I were dead. But in reality?" She smirked, savoring her twisted triumph. "We were more alive than ever."

I glared at Elizabeth, my body tense and my voice shaking with rage. "You call that living? Sacrificing your own son, turning your back on love and family, just for eternal life and wealth? You're not alive, Elizabeth. You're a hollow shell of a person, a monster."

At that moment, Ben struck me hard, and Frenchie bellowed in response. Ben grabbed my hair and forcibly dragged me into the center of the garden, but I wasn't going to make it easy for him. I bit his arm as hard as I could, but his hand neither bled nor seemed hurt. Seeing my wonder, he smirked, "Perks of making deals with demons. We don't get hurt."

He yanked my hair even harder, forcing me onto my knees in a prayer-like position. Then, he directed his gaze towards Elizabeth. With a wave of her hand, a book materialized out of thin air. As the book opened, a sudden gust of wind swirled around us, and the atmosphere grew dense. A shiver ran down my spine; I recognized this book. I had felt its energy before. It was a grimoire!

Chapter 25

ELIZABETH GRIPPED THE grimoire tightly, her chants growing louder until they morphed into an earth-shaking roar. The ground beneath us cracked open as if torn by an invisible hand, and flames burst forth, encircling us. Just then, a monstrous creature erupted from the fissure—its skin glowing like molten lava, eyes like dark voids, and horns so viciously sharp they seemed capable of slicing through solid rock.

Elizabeth met the demon's gaze and declared, "Great Balthazar, this sacrifice is for you!" Her hand gestured toward me, and as Balthazar's eyes locked onto mine, a jolt of terror coursed through my veins.

"A soul, so steeped in sadness and misery," the

demon murmured as it approached me, lifting my chin with its grotesque, talon-like nail. "Witch, you've chosen wisely this time," he commended Elizabeth.

As he raised his claw high, poised to strike me down, I mustered all the courage I had left. "Before you kill me, pay the debt," I blurted. His claw paused mid-air, and for a split second, time itself seemed to freeze.

I looked around and saw everything around us seemed still—the wind ceased its howling, and the world held its breath. While Elizabeth, Ben, and Frenchie stood frozen, like statues in the garden, I forced myself to my feet and looked up at the demon, as he towered over me.

"What debt?" Balthazar snarled, his voice dripping with menace. "Don't toy with me, witch."

.

"I'm not toying with you. I once saved your son, Balfeeral. Freed him from two centuries of agony. He owes me," I shot back, staring him down.

"He may owe you, but I owe you nothing. You think I'll just let a soul like yours go? Never!" The demon's voice thundered.

"So, blood pacts between demons and humans apply across human generations but not demonic ones? That's quite the double standard," I retorted. "Your son made a blood pact. That binds you as well, whether you like it or not."

The demon's roar cut through the silence, his eyes glaring like coals. "What do you want?" he hissed. My heart raced; I couldn't believe it. He was actually going to honor our pact.

Swallowing hard, I found my voice. "I want the souls freed. No more curse, no more torment. Let them rest."

He glanced at Elizabeth and Ben, their bodies frozen in time. "I have arrangements with those two," he growled, pointing a claw at them. His tone was menacing, but I sensed a moment of hesitation.

Taking a deep breath, I seized the opportunity. "What's more binding, a mere arrangement or a blood pact?"

His eyes narrowed, and for a moment, he bared his fangs in a snarl. "Very well," he finally hissed, as if conceding defeat. "At dawn, their souls will be freed."

"What about Frenchie? Will he be free too?" I

asked, the weight of my own hope hanging in the air.

"That's a different curse," he retorted. "The witch controls him. You must destroy her totem to release his soul."

"A totem?" I echoed, the word barely leaving my mouth before the demon vanished, as if swallowed by the earth itself and time unfroze.

When Elizabeth and Ben looked around and saw me, their faces twisted in disbelief and fury.

"Why is she still here? Ben, why is she still breathing?" Elizabeth's voice was full of desperation. She raised her hands to summon her magic, but when nothing happened, her face twisted in panic. "What did you do?" She shrieked, clawing at her own cheeks as if trying to rip away the disbelief.

Ben's eyes widened in horror. "What is it, my love?"

"My powers, Ben. Balthazar took back the powers he gave me!" Elizabeth cried out.

"Not just that Elizabeth, it's over. The curse on the manor has ended," I announced, triumphantly.

Ben's face twisted in rage as he locked eyes with

me. "You'll pay for this!" he snarled and lunged towards me but Frenchie was quicker. Suddenly freed from Elizabeth's magical hold, he stepped between us, and with a firm push sent Ben flying through the air. Ben hit the ground with a thud.

With a powerful swipe of his clawed hand, Frenchie broke the ropes that bound me. We stood there, side by side, against Elizabeth and Ben.

I kissed Frenchie. Our tongues met for a quick second, and it was like the world stopped. He bit my lip a little when we pulled away and then licked off the tiny bit of blood. "You taste like love," he said.

I looked right into his eyes. "And you feel like home," I said back. For a second, it was like nothing else mattered.

Then, snapping back to reality, Elizabeth's snarl pierced the moment. "How pathetic! Loving a monster who could never be anything but that."

I looked away from Frenchie, finally turning to her. "I don't care," I said, my eyes still lingering on him for a second longer. "But you, Elizabeth, you'll answer for everything you've done. Every single thing."

I locked eyes with Frenchie one more time. "I know what to do now, Frenchie. I can break the curse. The one that makes you a monster when darkness falls."

"I'll keep them busy. Go," he said.

With a quick nod, I turned and ran, my mind buzzing with the plan. Every step took me closer to ending this nightmare for good.

Chapter 26

AS SOON AS Balthazar had mentioned a totem, things clicked, just as I had suspected. The peculiar marks on Frenchie when he turned into a monster weren't random; they were spells. Elizabeth had used his body as a cursed object. A totem. I had to destroy it to free him.

Armed with a gas lamp I took from the cottage, I dashed to the cemetery. My light danced over the graves as I ran past them. My mind traveled to the vision I had at the manor. It wasn't me marking Frenchie's body; it was, in fact, Elizabeth. I had seen the vision through her eyes. Her words rang in my mind, 'He will be with his son now.' That was it! Frenchie was buried with his son Peter. That grave held the totem.

I sped up, every step urgent. Time was running out. I had to get to that grave, find the totem, and smash it.

I zeroed in on the oak tree, Frenchie's favorite spot. That's where Peter's grave was. My hands dove into the soil near the tree, ripping it away. My fingers hurt, but I kept going. Every handful of dirt took me closer to ending the curse. I needed to find that totem now. I continued to dig with my hands, tearing through the cold, damp earth until they bled.

My heart pounded as I jumped into the hole. With fast scoops, I cleared more dirt. Soon, I found a coffin just below the surface. Inside was Frenchie, covered in symbols. Next to him was a smaller skeleton—his son Peter. Tears filled my eyes seeing them like this, stuck together even in death.

I got out of the hole and reached for my lantern. Just then, something yanked my hair hard. I turned around. It was Elizabeth.

"You think you can just waltz in and ruin everything, Evelynn?" she snarled, smashing my head against the hard ground. Stars exploded across my vision.

I wasn't about to let her get the better of me. Mustering all my strength, I kicked her hard in the stomach. She went flying back, arms flailing. "This ends now, Elizabeth!"

Still reeling, she got up and lunged at me, her sharp nails aiming for my eyes. I rolled with her on top of me, and once she was beneath me, I seized the opportunity to head-butt her. Dazed, she released her grip.

With her momentarily stunned, I grabbed her arm and hauled her over to Peter's grave. "I hope you rot here," I spat, pushing her into the open hole.

Screams ripped from her throat as she tried to claw her way out. A well-placed kick sent her sprawling back onto the coffin, her face a mask of dirt and rage.

Fumbling for a moment, I regained my grip on the lantern. Its flickering flame seemed to dance in tune with my racing heartbeat. "May you find the hell you so richly deserve, Elizabeth."

I let go of the lantern and it fell into the grave, breaking on impact. Oil from the lamp spilled over Elizabeth and the ground. For a second, everything was still. Then, the small flame from the broken lantern met the oil.

Watching the fire snake its way towards Elizabeth, the gravity of the moment hit me hard. Her screams filled the air, and I found my voice.

"Elizabeth," I shouted over the roar of the flames, "this is the end you've written for yourself! You played with lives as if they were your personal chess pieces! With Fredrick, with Peter, with me! You thought you could bend the world to your dark whims. Not anymore!"

As the fire grew, consuming her, my words seemed to blend with the crackling and popping of the flames. I continued, my voice filled with a heavy sense of finality, "May you understand in death what you never grasped in life: the consequences of your actions. May your spirit find no rest, just as you gave none!"

Her scream was cut off, swallowed by the fire, as if even the flames wouldn't allow her the finality of a last word. I stood there, my eyes wet but my heart steadfast, watching until the fire had done its job and burned itself out. This chapter was closed. The nightmare was finally over.

Chapter 27

STAGGERING BACK INTO the garden, the world felt distorted. The few statues that remained in the garden were now broken. Everything was a mess.

Ben's screams pierced the night. I rushed toward the source of the commotion and saw Frenchie straddling Ben, relentlessly pummeling him.

Struggling for breath, Ben managed to croak, "You... you can't... do this..."

But Frenchie was relentless, his voice filled with a burning fury. "I can, Ben," he hissed, "You caused me so much pain. My son, the innocent souls trapped in this forsaken place, and most of all, Evelynn."

I slowly walked towards them. As Frenchie

continued to hit him, Ben's blood splattered, some of it landing on me.

Ben, his voice trembling, begged for mercy, "Please... mercy... I'm sorry..."

Frenchie's smile widened as he continued his relentless assault. "Sorry won't save you now, Ben. Evelynn suffered because of you." With a final, devastating strike, he crushed Ben's skull, bringing an end to the torment that had plagued us for so long.

Frenchie stood up and I looked at Ben's body with a dark satisfaction, knowing that it was all over now.

Frenchie's eyes met mine, scanning my face— covered in blood, but to him, beautiful. "You've never looked more captivating," he said, relief and awe coloring his voice. "Red really suits you."

He closed the distance between us and kissed me. For a moment, everything else faded away; it was just us, frozen in a world that had seen too much horror but was now strangely quiet. Finally, he pulled back, still locking eyes with me.

I gazed at him, my voice barely more than a whisper, "So what happens now?"

His fingers gently traced the curve of my cheek as he spoke, his words laced with a profound desire, "I don't know all the answers, Evelynn, but I do know one thing. I want to be with you. Forever."

My heart swelled at his words, and I couldn't help but ask, "How, Frenchie?"

Dropping to one knee, Frenchie looked up at me, his eyes still glowing with their otherworldly intensity, yet softened by vulnerability. "Will you be the one good thing in this dark, haunted place? Will you marry me?"

His unexpected question left me momentarily stunned, and I couldn't help but let out a surprised chuckle.

"Say yes, and I promise, all the darkness will have been worth it," Frenchie's voice was a mix of raw need and hope.

"Yes," I whispered, sealing our haunted fairy tale. He scooped me up, his arms sturdy as bedrock, and carried me back into the manor.

We passed through the towering doorway, down the hallway, and Frenchie didn't stop until we reached the bedroom. Those azure eyes of his were ablaze, as if he'd just conquered some ferocious beast. He lowered me onto the bed and then filled the bathtub with warm water. "You're a masterpiece, you know," he mumbled as his hands peeled off my soiled clothes, "A beautiful, complex work of art."

He lifted me into the warm water. My skin buzzed as he began to wash away the grime and blood, each touch deliberate, each kiss a promise. "Every inch of you is perfect to me," he whispered, lips grazing my collarbone, making my pulse quicken.

"Don't know about perfect," I said, looking away.

"Trust me, you are," he insisted, pulling me back to meet his gaze. The time in the tub felt endless and too short all at once.

Draped in towels, we stepped out of the bathroom. In the closet, I found a white dress, simple but elegant. Slipping it on, I felt a combination of joyful and nervous.

Frenchie stood behind me, his fingers deftly lacing up the back of the dress. "You look breathtaking," he murmured, his lips leaving a soft, lingering kiss on my shoulder.

"But who's going to marry us?" I finally asked, breaking a long, passionate kiss.

Frenchie chuckled. "Remember, we've got a priest among the resident ghosts. A spectral wedding for a love that conquered horror? Sounds perfect to me."

I turned and our eyes met, and in that moment, everything felt exactly as it should be—hauntingly perfect.

Chapter 28

T HE MANOR HAD a different kind of beauty tonight, lit up by candles and gas lamps. Chloe had played a big part in this transformation. Chloe had taken the knife from her ghostly husband, sending him running with a look only a scorned woman can give. With the same knife, she also skillfully cut and shaped an old tablecloth, turning it into the charming veil that I now wore. I felt its soft touch against my back as I started down the makeshift aisle towards Frenchie. The flickering candles and glowing gas lamps bathed the room in a hauntingly beautiful light.

Frenchie stood at the end of the aisle, his eyes shining with emotion. "You are a vision," he whispered as I reached him, taking my hands into his.

The ghostly priest stepped in front of us. "We stand here, in the realm that veers between the living and the dead, to bind two souls eternally," he intoned, his voice like a cold wind that somehow still warmed me. "Do you, Frenchie, take Evelynn to be your bride, in this life and the ones beyond, through light that pierces the gloom and shadows that swallow the moon?"

"I do," Frenchie's voice resonated, like a chant.

"And do you, Evelynn, accept Frenchie to be your phantom groom, in this realm and the nether, under sun's blaze and in the obsidian dark?"

"I do," I replied, my voice a whisper, as though speaking too loudly might shatter the delicate fabric of this haunted moment.

"Very well," the ghostly priest nodded. "Now, let your vows echo through the veils of reality, time, and decay."

Frenchie's eyes locked onto mine, as if he could see straight into my soul. "I vow to be your sentinel in the moonlight and your companion in the gloom. To stand with you when the banshees howl and the dark spirits loom. Our love will be the light that even shadows dare not consume."

Moved by his words, I took a deep breath. "I vow to be your haven amidst hauntings, your sanctuary in the supernatural. I'll stand by you when the phantoms whisper and when the cursed objects stir. Our love will defy both spectral chill and the heat of the liveliest fire."

With a final nod, the ghostly priest murmured, "Then by the powers that haunt these walls, and the energies that bind us all, I pronounce you bound in matrimony, in the mortal realm and the spectral beyond. You may now seal this union with a kiss."

Our lips met, and in that instant, the air around us felt electrified, as if the very spirits that haunted these halls were lifting their spectral glasses in a toast to our eternal love.

Chapter 29

THE BALLROOM HAD shifted from a cavern of haunts to our own sacred haven. Gone were the ominous shadows; now it was as if the very walls celebrated our love. The room danced in the soft glow of flickering candles. The blended aroma of burnt wax and timeworn wood hung in the air, comforting in its familiarity. The air itself felt like a loving embrace, heavy yet soothing. And there we were, lost in each other's eyes, as we moved to an invisible melody, our feet hardly making contact with the floor's ancient boards.

Then, a glow. I caught sight of Frenchie's palm emitting a golden radiance. Snapping out of our love-infused trance, I looked around. Other spirits in the room were glowing too—each their own shade of ethereal light. The air tensed up, as if holding its own breath in anticipation.

"It's time," Chloe whispered, her eyes locked on her husband, whose glow had turned an ominous gray. "You're destined for a much darker place, my dear." With that, she disappeared, and her husband's screams filled the room, a wail so disturbing it seemed to penetrate my very bones. And just like that, he was gone too—absorbed into a void.

The room began to empty, spirits fading away like morning mist, as if being gently pulled back into the universe's embrace. Then I saw something startling. Even though Elizabeth and Ben had been killed outside the manor, their bodies were being dragged inside. It was as if the portal to the other side existed within the manor itself. Chains materialized around their wrists, pulling them toward a yawning abyss. Their screams were terrifying, their faces contorted in anguish, eyes bulging in helpless dread.

My focus snapped back to Frenchie. My eyes were wet, vision blurred. The golden glow in his palm was now faint, as if resisting its fate. His eyes met mine—so full of sorrow they nearly broke me.

"I can't bear to leave you," Frenchie's voice was shaky with a desperation that struck me to my core.

"You have to, Frenchie. You've suffered for so long. You deserve peace." my voice was a fragile whisper, trembling as I fought back tears.

"I won't ever lose you," he vowed, his grip on my hands tightening as if he were anchoring himself to this world through me. "Even heaven wouldn't be enough if you're not with me."

"Well, then I'll end this life and join you. What's the point of living if you're not in it?" My voice quivered with emotion.

Frenchie's face was a swirl of emotion—love, pain, and resolve. "Evelynn, listen to me. Ava's still out there, living her life. You've got to live for her, and for yourself. Promise me you'll live a long, happy life. Do it for me."

Struggling to keep my voice steady, I managed to say, "I promise."

Our foreheads touched, sealing the vow.

Finally, I pulled away, heart heavy but full of purpose. I left the manor, driven by the newfound mission to reunite with Ava, my lost daughter. Frenchie stayed behind, his spectral presence lingering like a guardian angel, fueled by a love that would wait for me through centuries, if it had to. "I'll be right here, waiting for you, no matter how long it takes," his words echoed in my mind as I stepped into the world, forever changed.

Epilogue

AS I LAY there, coughing and wiping the sweat from my brow, Ava's concerned voice reached me.

"Mummy, are you alright?" she asked with worry in her voice.

I managed to respond, though each breath felt heavier than the last. "Yes, I... I..." Another cough interrupted my feeble attempt to reassure her.

"I think it's time," I whispered, my voice trembling. Ava, my dear child, took my hand, her tears glistening in her eyes.

Mark, her loving husband, stepped forward to help me up. With his support, I managed to rise from the bed. Casey and Tom, Ava's children, leaned in to kiss me on the cheek, their youthful innocence contrasting the gravity of the moment.

Ava and Mark guided me through the familiar corridors of the manor, my steps growing weaker with each passing moment. Finally, we reached the bedroom, where I lay down, taking heavy breaths as the weight of the years settled upon me.

My mind drifted back to the day I had left the manor, seeking a life with Ava once more. Mr. and Mrs. Darcy had been instrumental in helping us reunite. Frenchie, my beloved, had provided me with jewels from the manor, which I had sold to secure the means to start fresh. Edward tried to slither back into my life when he got wind that I had some money, but I promptly kicked him out. Later, I heard he suffered a long, agonizing death from tuberculosis. It felt like justice.

I had never left my role as the caretaker of the manor. Even though Lady Cassandra had attempted to rent it out, Frenchie made sure that it remained unoccupied. I continued to reside in the cottage with Ava, and every night, I met my husband. Though Ava couldn't see him, she felt his presence.

Thirty years had passed since the day I married Frenchie, and now, as an old woman, it was time to embrace the inevitable. I chose to spend my final moments in the manor, where my husband had patiently awaited my final return for so long.

Ava leaned down, her kiss a mixture of love and sorrow, and as life began to leave my body, I felt a profound sense of peace. My soul began its journey, leaving behind my earthly form. When my eyes closed for the last time, I saw him—Frenchie—radiant in a way I had never seen before.

My hands, once marked by the passage of time, were now smooth and unblemished. I was the age I had been when I first met Frenchie, our love still fresh and new.

"Frenchie," I whispered, my voice filled with longing. He smiled, his eyes filled with a depth of emotion that transcended the physical realm. "Evelynn, my dearest."

Our lips met in a kiss that held the essence of a love that had endured through time and trials. It was a kiss that bridged the gap between two worlds, a testament to the eternal nature of our connection. As we embraced in that otherworldly realm, the weight of age and suffering lifted, leaving only the purest form of our love.

Acknowledgements

I'd like to give a big shout-out to my husband, the no-nonsense software engineer, who somehow manages to keep up with my goth girl shenanigans. You've always encouraged me to chase my dreams, even when it involves monsters and spooky tales. You're my real-life hero.

To the fantastic Facebook groups out there that revel in dark romance and all things gothic, you've been my partners in crime when it comes to finding the spookiest and most thrilling reads. Thanks for the recommendations and the lively discussions.

And let's not forget the dark romance authors who've made me swoon, shiver, and scribble down my own tales. You've rocked my world with your words!

So, a massive thanks to my hubby and these incredible dark romance authors, and the entire dark romance squad for inspiring me to embrace my spooky side and write on.

With love and monsters,

Sephyrra.

Connect with the
Author

How to Help an Indie Author

If you want to keep indie stories alive (and keep me caffeinated), here's how you can help:

- **Leave a review.** Even a quick line on Amazon, Goodreads, or BookBub helps more than you know.

- **Tell a friend.** Hand a book to someone who needs a little monster romance in their life.

- **Share online.** Post quotes, selfies with the book, or reactions on social media. Tag me so I can flail over it.

- **Request my books.** Ask your local bookstore or library to stock them.

- **Check out my Etsy shop.** Signed bookplates, extras, and monster merch live there.

- **Stay connected.** My newsletter, Facebook group, and Discord are the best way to get early reveals and chaos.